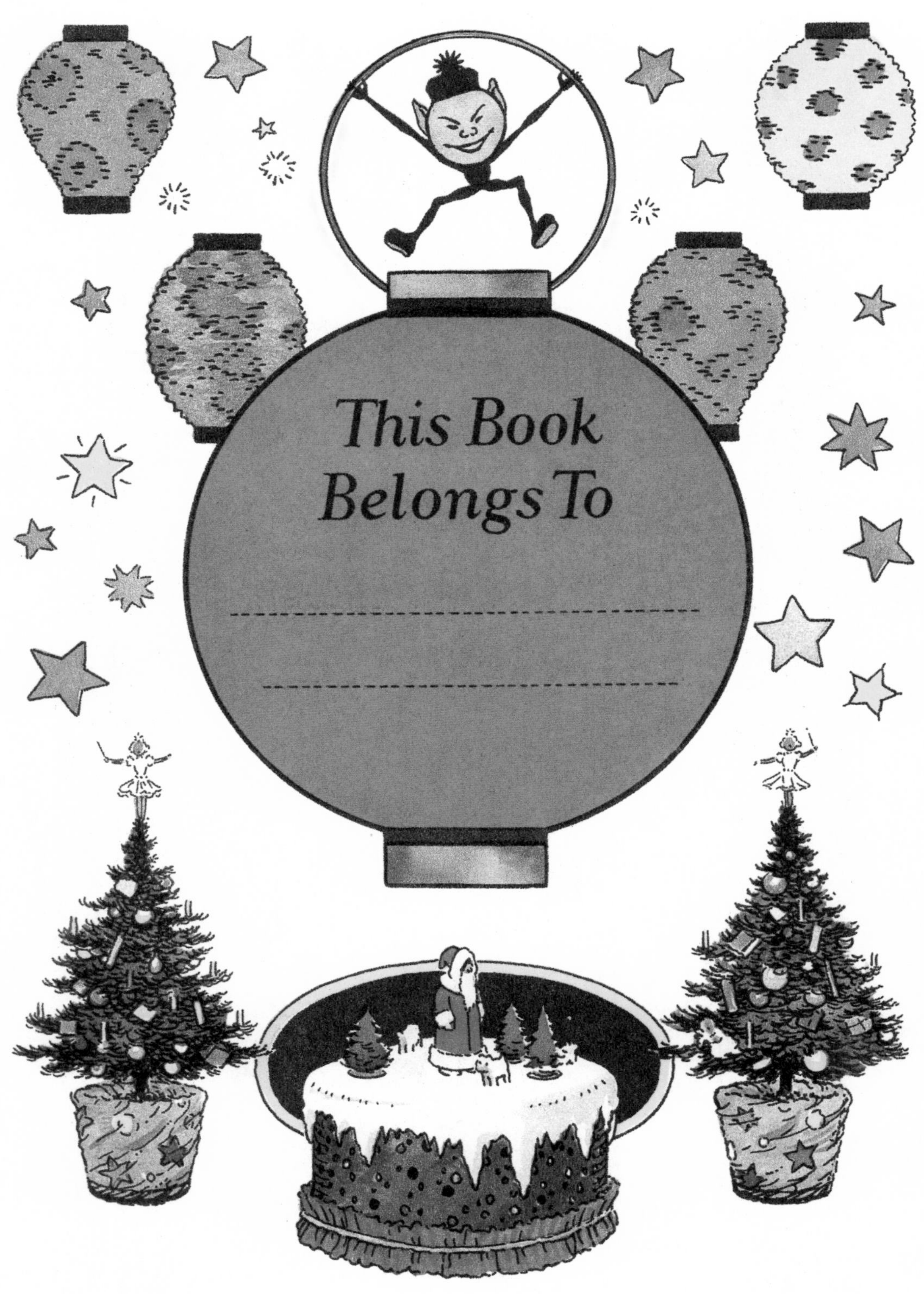

Original edition published 1957.
This facsimile edition printed by Leo Paper, China.
Colour Reproduction by Scriveners Reprographics, Totnes, Devon.

RUPERT

A DAILY EXPRESS PUBLICATION

8704

Printed in Great Britain

4'6

RUPERT'S PAINTING PUZZLE

The black-and-white picture is ready for you to colour. Look carefully at the shapes beside the picture and find out where the pieces fit into the scene, just as if they were parts of a jigsaw puzzle. Some of the shapes are turned around, so you may find it easier to look at them from different ways. Paint the picture piece by piece, copying the colour of each shape, and soon your painting will look very pretty.

CONTENTS

RUPERT and the

There is trouble when a naugh

Says Rupert to his little chum,
" Now why has that white doggie come ? "

" He's brought a note. I can't make out
What all these squiggles are about."

RUPERT is out walking one cold winter's day soon after Christmas. He leaves the village of Nutwood and makes for the open country. As he climbs a grassy slope he meets his friend Rastus, the country mouse, resting by a tree. " Thank you for your Christmas card, Rastus," says the little bear. " It was very pretty." " So was yours, Rupert," replies the little mouse. " Did you have lots of presents ? " " Oh, rather," says Rupert, and he begins to tell his chum about the nice surprises he found in his stocking on Christmas morning. Suddenly Rastus cuts him short. " Hey, look what's coming ! " he exclaims. " Whose little animal is that ? " For a small white dog is running down a bank straight towards them. In his mouth is an envelope which he drops at Rupert's feet. " Is this meant for me ? " asks the little bear. He takes the letter out and frowns. " Oh dear, I can't understand this," he murmurs. " There are no words here—only weird marks."

CRACKER JACK

mp from China is set free by mistake

" If we can keep the dog in sight,"
Says Rupert, " he may lead us right."

Then Tigerlily shows her face
Above her nearby hiding place.

Rastus catches a glimpse of the strange writing, and he shakes his head in bewilderment. " It is all squiggles and zig-zags," he says. " Someone must have written it for a joke." The chums look down at the little dog who sits up and gives a sharp " Woof ! " " He seems to be asking for something," remarks Rastus. " Perhaps he is waiting for an answer." " Well, I can't send one, because I can't read this letter," says Rupert. " I am not even sure that it was meant for me. My name was not on the envelope. And anyway, where did the dog come from ? " At last the dog trots away, still watched by the chums. " Let's keep him in sight," says Rastus. " We may see who sent him." As they follow the dog past some bushes they are startled by a cheery " Coo-ee ! " " Who was that ? " gasps Rastus, turning round quickly. " There's no one in sight—ooh ! " He hops behind Rupert as the mischievous face of Tigerlily appears smiling above the branches.

RUPERT SEES A PAPER GLIDER

She says, " In Chinese words I wrote
My little invitation note."

" Hoorah ! " shouts Willie in great glee.
" We'll find some pals to share the tea ! "

The chums meet Edward Trunk, and so
They ask him if he'd like to go.

And as they hurry down the lane,
They see a tiny paper 'plane.

" Hello," says Rupert as the little Chinese girl comes forward. " Is that your white doggie? And this letter, was it meant for me? I can't read a word of it." " Yes, yes, him my doggie," laughs Tigerlily. " And me play joke on you. That letter is invitation all written in Chinese. You find some pals and come tea with me today to meet my cousin Ting Ling, just from China. You come, yes? Good, me go now." And she trots away. " This should be fun," cries Rupert, " we'll round up our pals. Look, there's Edward. Let's ask him to join us." Rupert then unfolds the strange letter and, showing it to Edward, he tells him of Tigerlily's joke and of her invitation. " I'd like to be in on this," Edward smiles. As they walk along together a small, light object glides gently over their heads. " What ever is that?" says Rastus. " It looks like a tiny delta-winged 'plane." " We're just passing Bingo's house," says Rupert. " Let's ask if that thing is his."

RUPERT INVITES BINGO THE PUP

It's one of Bingo's latest things
And Rupert says, " I like the wings."

" Oh, Bingo, will you come with me
To Tigerlily's house for tea ? "

Says Mrs. Bear, "Before you start
You'd better make yourselves look smart."

Then arm in arm, all in a row,
They say goodbye, and off they go.

Just then Bingo, the brainy pup, appears from his house. " Hullo, you chaps," he calls. " How do you like that thing? I've been inventing paper gliders and that's a jolly good one." " Yes, it does fly well," says Rupert, " but never mind that for the moment. We've come to ask you out to tea." When Bingo hears of Tigerlily's invitation he, too, promises to join the others in the afternoon and they agree where to meet. Rupert and Rastus and Edward find Algy Pug and Podgy Pig and tell them of the invitation. Then they go to Rupert's cottage. " We'd better not take *too* many," says the little bear. " Six is enough. And Tigerlily didn't say it was to be a party, so we needn't put on our party clothes." " No, but you must see that your boots are clean," says Mrs. Bear when she hears where they are going. " And mind you all wash carefully behind your ears ! " So in the afternoon Bingo joins them and they set off towards the Conjuror's house.

RUPERT MEETS TING LING

The Chinese cousins bow to greet
The playmates whom they come to meet.

Then smiling Ting Ling says with pride,
" I show you something ! Come inside ! "

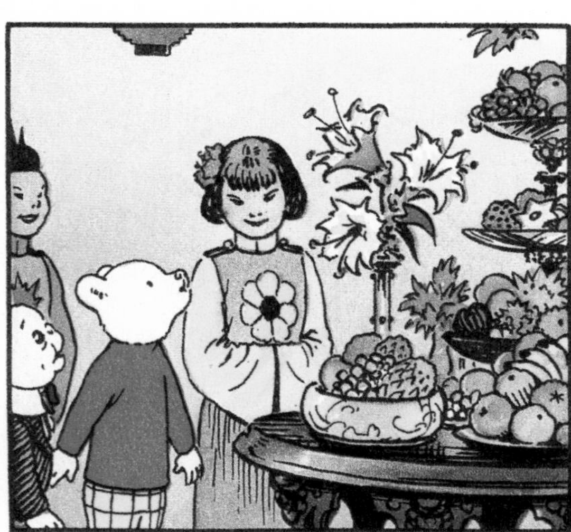

And when they see the table there,
The friends can only stand and stare.

" More wonders we see in a while,"
Says Tigerlily with a smile.

Tigerlily and her cousin await the arrival of their guests and Ting Ling bows politely as the group of little friends stand shyly before him. One by one, the pals are introduced to him and he tries to call them by their names. " Ah, there is Lupert the little bear," he says. " Me hear often of you, me likee walk with you and we go indoors now please. Then me show something interesting me bring from China." And indoors they all go. After the little friends have taken off their coats and scarves Tigerlily invites them into a room. " Whew, just look at those lovely things ! " çries Rupert as they stop before a low table loaded with rare fruit and wonderful flowers. " We didn't know it was to be this sort of party or we should have put on our best clothes for it." " No need worry," Tigerlily smiles. " We not want party clo'es. Ting Ling fetch all nice t'ings from China. Now he wants to show somet'ing even more wonderful." And Ting Ling leads the way.

RUPERT IS SHOWN A TRICK

They gather round with wondering eyes,
And watch the smoke curl up and rise.

Then Podgy starts to sneeze, " At-choo !
Why Rupert ! Algy ! Where are you ? "

But soon the smoke is not so thick
And Ting Ling goes on with his trick.

And when the air is clear once more,
A cracker settles on the floor.

The little friends wait eagerly. " If Ting Ling can show us anything more wonderful than that table full of fruit he must be clever," whispers Rupert. Gathering round, they watch carefully as the Chinese boy pours drops into a glass of curious form. Then he adds powder and immediately faint smoke curls upward and spreads under the ceiling. Gradually the whole room becomes misty as the sweet-smelling fumes swirl about. " Here, where has everyone gone ? " wheezes Podgy. " I can't see any more." While Rupert and his pals are trying to find their way out of the fog and getting rather frightened it quickly thins out and they see Ting Ling. Above him a large shape appears slowly from the mist and settles gently on the floor. " Oh look, it's a Christmas cracker. What a whopper ! " cries Rupert. " How can anyone pull it ? " " No need pull clacker," smiles Ting Ling. " Him full of Chinee magic. Me show you."

RUPERT GETS A TEASING

" Inside are gifts for everyone,
When it go bang, we have some fun ! "

The cracker goes off with a crash,
And then they see a blinding flash.

" What imp is this ? " cries Rupert Bear,
" Who pinches us and pulls our hair ? "

" It's my mistake ! This naughty thing
Is bad, bad magic ! " gasps Ting Ling.

Wondering what the Chinese boy is going to do, Rupert and the others stand back and gaze at the huge cracker. " Chinee clacker velly good clacker," says Ting Ling. " Him full of nice plesents, plesents for all of us. Now you watch. Me make um go bang." He waves his hands over the cracker, muttering queer outlandish words, and to everybody's astonishment it rises quivering from the floor. Suddenly there is a loud bang and a blinding flash, the magic cracker splits and vanishes, and out of the flash is tossed a small dark object. When the light smoke from the explosion drifts away all is confusion. The little object that flew from the cracker can now be seen clearly, a sort of imp with a large head and skinny arms and legs. He flips about in the air teasing people, pinching their ears and pulling their hair, while Bingo has his spectacles snatched from his nose. "Oh dear, me make mistake," cries Ting Ling. " Me make velly bad magic clacker ! "

RUPERT HEARS ABOUT THE IMP

" No gifts for us," sighs Rastus Mouse ,
" Why did *that imp come to this house?"*

Says Tigerlily, " Me afraid
One plenty big mistake was made."

Then Ting Ling says, " Bad, news, I fear
The Crackerjack, him disappear ! "

Quite suddenly the imp turns up
And starts to tease the little pup.

When the little creature has seized the spectacles it darts from the room with the Chinese boy after it. " But what *is* it ? " cries Rupert. " Ting Ling said we should all get presents out of the cracker." " Yes, yes," says Tigerlily anxiously, " only he make bad magic and bad clacker. Instead of plesents out come Chinee Clackerjack. Him no good, Chinee Imp of Mischief, velly naughty, must catch at once or him do big damages. Come, we help Ting Ling chase and catchee." At that moment Ting Ling returns looking very worried. " Him disappear," he says breathlessly. " Clacker-jack go vanish. Me no catchee." But while he speaks there is a scuffle in a passage and from another door a small white animal bolts across the room closely pursued by the Crackerjack. He is no longer holding Bingo's spectacles and has found a new form of mischief in trying to pull the little dog's tail. " Quick, we must stop him," Rupert calls. " That poor doggie's scared."

RUPERT CHASES THE CRACKERJACK

"Quick," Rupert gasps. "Keep him in sight–
That doggie's having such a fright."

Says Edward Trunk, "I cannot hear
The slightest sound! That's very queer!"

"Me t'ink we search now, two by two,
It quite the best t'ing we can do."

Then Rupert hears poor Bingo call,
"Oh dear! I cannot see at all!"

With Rupert in the lead the friends dash off in pursuit of the mischievous Crackerjack. Out of the room they go and down more passages, but no one can get near him. The sound of the dog barking takes them to a distant part of the house and then they gather in a group to listen. "No noise now and no more barking," whispers Tigerlily. "My little doggie get teased and he no like it." "This is queer," says Edward. "I've got big ears and even I cannot hear anything now." Ting Ling is getting so very anxious that Tigerlily decides to order the search properly. "My house bigger than you t'ink," she says. "We must divide and go two by two different ways. Then maybe we find." She hurries off with Ting Ling, leaving the little pals to sort themselves out. All at once Rupert hears a plaintive call behind him and looking round he sees Bingo standing helplessly. "I can't help," says Bingo. "I can't see properly. The Crackerjack took my specs."

RUPERT FINDS THE GLASSES

" To take your specs was very bad,
But we'll soon find them ! Don't be sad."

They haven't gone back very far,
When Rupert cries, " Look ! Here they are ! "

" Good, now I've got my glasses back,
I'll help you find the Crackerjack ! "

Says Rupert, " We are left behind.
Let's search and see what we can find."

" I'd forgotten about your losing your specs," says Rupert, " when we last saw the Crackerjack he wasn't holding them. He must have dropped them somewhere. Let's search." Carefully he leads the way right back to their starting point. As he glances around the room Rupert gives a start. " Why, there they are ! " he cries. " The Crackerjack must have popped them into this lovely bowl of fruit while he chased the doggie ! " Bingo is overjoyed to get his spectacles back. " I can hardly believe that they're safe and sound," he smiles. " Now I'm as good as anybody. What shall I do next ? " " Well, the others have paired off and gone to search for the Crackerjack," replies Rupert. " So you and I had better be partners and search in another direction." They move quietly into the passage and listen. " I can't hear anything of the other pairs. Perhaps they're searching the gardens," he adds. " We can look where we like."

RUPERT GOES ON A SEARCH

The pals soon hear a muffled sound,
" What's that ? " says Rupert, turning round.

" I think we ought to go and see,
So come on, Bingo, follow me ! "

They climb the stairs, flight after flight,
Until a landing comes in sight.

They hear the whining sound once more,
And stand and listen at the door.

The two pals move as silently as they can, often stopping to listen for any sound from the Crackerjack or from the other pairs who are searching. For some time all is silence. Then at the bottom of a small stairway Rupert stops. " My ears are very keen," he mutters. " I'm sure there was a tiny noise from up there. It's the first sound we've heard, so let's follow it whatever it was." They start gingerly and find themselves on a rather dark winding staircase that goes up and up and up until it reaches a landing high up in the building. " I can hear that sound more clearly now," says Rupert. " It's like the whining of a dog. We must be on the right track. The Crackerjack was chasing the little white dog when we last saw him. I believe he's in here." He puts his ear to a door. " Is that door locked ? " asks Bingo. " It doesn't matter if it is," says Rupert. " The key's here on the outside. Come on, we'd better go in and look for him."

Rupert and the Crackerjack

RUPERT SCAMPERS AROUND

" I see him ! " cries the little bear.
" Beneath that cupboard over there ! "

Above their heads the creature flicks,
And starts his old, annoying tricks.

No sooner has the chase begun
The doggie sees his chance to run.

" The imp ! I've caught him ! " Bingo calls,
Then suddenly he trips and falls.

Rupert opens the door and peeps into an untidy room with boxes and papers strewn about. At first he thinks the room is empty, then he sees that the little white dog is crouching under a carved cupboard while the grinning Crackerjack is perched on top. " He's here," Rupert calls. " Let's try and get him to come with us to Tiger-lily." But as soon as he and Bingo move forward the Crackerjack starts its old tricks, flicking itself through the air always just out of their reach. The two pals chase it round and round the room, making the place still more untidy, but the more they puff and pant the more the little creature jeers at them. Meanwhile, the little dog, seeing the door open, seizes his chance to bolt unnoticed by Rupert. However, the Crackerjack has seen him and he too darts out of the room. In a last despairing effort to grab him Bingo trips over a stool and goes sprawling. " I don't believe *anyone* can catch him," gasps Rupert.

RUPERT AND BINGO ARE TRAPPED

" The door won't open ! Goodness me !
That creature must have turned the key ! "

So neatly trapped, they start to shout
And hope their friends will get them out.

But though they shout and shout again
They realise it's all in vain.

Says Rupert, " I know what to do !
This window opens—let's look through ! "

After the Crackerjack has disappeared the door slams and the two pals hardly notice that there is an extra click until they try to get out of the room. " I say, I can't open this," cries Rupert. " That horrid little creature must have locked us in ! I told you the key was on the outside." He bangs on the door until his knuckles are sore and then Bingo joins him. " We'd better shout for help. Someone may hear us and come up to set us free," he says. " Now both together — Help, HELP ! " Rupert and Bingo become frightened when their shouts bring no answer from anybody. " We may be prisoners for ages before anyone finds us," Bingo quavers. " D'you think we could make a hole in the floor and call down through that ? " " No, I'm sure we couldn't," says Rupert slowly. " I've a better idea than that. There's a window at the other end of the room. Let's see if any of the others are in the grounds. We may be able to let them know we're trapped."

RUPERT SHOUTS FOR HELP

He pushes back the window wide,
But cannot see their friends outside.

Once more they try to call their chums
But though they wait nobody comes.

At last a little group is near,
Croaks Rupert, " Bingo, make them hear ! "

" We've shouted far too much, of course,
And that is what has made us hoarse ! "

Rupert manages to open the window. " Take care, we mustn't fall out," he warns. " We're very high up. I can see a lot of the grounds from here. If only there were some of our pals in sight. Still, some of them may be down there hidden by bushes, so we shall have to yell again." " Oh dear, *must* we ? I'm getting quite weak," says Bingo. " All right, let's try again." And together they look from the window and shout as loudly as they can. Then after a rest they shout and shout and shout again. After a time Rupert finds he is very hoarse " Oh my," he thinks. " Nobody could hear me." At that moment small figures appear in the garden far below. He waves frantically, but they do not look up. " I say, Bingo, there's somebody in sight and I've lost my voice. Why aren't you shouting ? " he wheezes. But his pal isn't there. Bingo is the other side of the room looking scared. " I've lost my voice too," he croaks. " We've both shouted too much."

Rupert and the Crackerjack

RUPERT WRITES A MESSAGE

" Oh dear ! What ever can we do ?
I'm much too tired to think, aren't you ? "

Cries Rupert, " I know how to bring
Our friends—this is the very thing ! "

" I'll write a message to explain,
And you can make a paper 'plane."

" I hope you're getting on all right.
Do hurry, while they're still in sight ! "

The two pals sit and look miserably at each other. " I couldn't raise another shout if I tried ever so," Bingo breathes rustily. " And I feel so *tired.*" " Yes, we're in a real fix," Rupert whispers. He gazes round at the untidy room, then he stiffens slightly and picks up a piece of paper. " Do you remember your paper glider ? " his voice remains hoarse. " Can you still make it ? Could you make one to fly straight ? " " Why, yes, of course I could," gasps Bingo. " Have you got another of your ideas ? " Rupert is quickly at work. " What luck that I have a pencil in my pocket," he murmurs. " I'm going to write a message on several of these odd bits of paper. Then you make them into your special gliders and we'll send them down when we see people in the grounds." Bingo loses no time in falling in with the plan. " I'll soon make you some fine gliders," he promises. " Well, hurry up," Rupert is now at the window, " there are more people in sight."

Rupert and the Crackerjack

RUPERT IS FREE AT LAST

They look and see their friends still there,
Then launch the glider in the air.

"What's that above us?" Edward cries,
As overhead the glider flies.

They stand and listen by the door,
And know they'll soon be out once more.

The two are very glad to see
Their friends who come to set them free.

When preparations are done Rupert makes way for Bingo at the window and the brainy pup carefully launches his first glider. In quiet air it wobbles once or twice and then sets off on a long straight glide over bushes and over the heads of Tigerlily and Ting Ling and just over Edward and Algy. "Look there's another of Bingo's gliders," says Edward. "Where has it come from? Let's grab it." And afar off Rupert, to his delight, sees them pick it up and examine it. Edward and Algy see Rupert's writing on the paper glider and then they spy their two pals at the high window. "Now we shan't be trapped much longer," says Rupert huskily. "What luck! The very first glider we sent down did the trick!" He listens at the door. "Someone's coming," he whispers. The key turns and they are free. "Well, well," cries Tigerlily. "How come you lock yourselves in up here?" "We didn't!" Rupert wheezes. "That naughty Crackerjack locked us in!"

RUPERT GASPS AT THE DAMAGE

And when they get their voices back,
They ask about the Crackerjack.

" I'm sure that noise means something's crashed !
Yes, look ! This lovely vase is smashed ! "

The shouts, the scuffle and the din
Bring the Chinese Conjuror in.

At last the Conjuror sits down,
And listens with an anxious frown.

As their voices gradually return Rupert and Bingo tell how they found the dog and the mischievous Crackerjack in the top room and how they lost them again. " I hope you've managed to catch that Crackerjack by now," says Rupert. " No, we no catchee," moans Tigerlily. " Him make great troubles and damages all over house." As she speaks there is a crash and running to another room they find the ruins of a beautiful vase and an overturned table. While Rupert and his friends are looking shocked at the breakage another sound makes them turn sharply. There in the doorway they see the stern figure of the Chinese Conjuror, Tigerlily's daddy. " And what mean this so tellible noise when me trying to work ? " he demands. " And who smash valuable Ming vase. And why all these little animals dashing about my house ? " As he sits down and looks grim, Ting Ling hurries to tell him all about the cracker and the Crackerjack.

Rupert and the Crackerjack

RUPERT WATCHES THE CONJUROR

*" Move back and leave the floor quite clear
And watch me catchee creature here ! "*

*Thinks Rupert, " It's some magic spell,
But how it works, I cannot tell ! "*

*And in the smoke clouds they can see
A strange glass jar ! What can it be ?*

*" The Crackerjack is back with us ! "
Cries Bingo. " Will he cause more fuss ? "*

When he hears what has happened the Conjuror looks more severe than ever. He rises and waves Rupert and his friends away. " Leave all floor clear," he commands. " This velly, velly bad business. Crackerjack may break up house. Must find at once. Him full of Chinee magic so nobody can catchee. Must use still stronger Chinee magic. All stand back and you watchee me catchee." He marks out a circle and fetches a lot of small pointed objects which he arranges in a magic shape. When his preparations are done the Conjuror sets light to all the little cones and right in the middle of the circle he puts a large jar without a lid. Then he stands back waving his wand and saying weird Chinese spells. Rupert and the others watch while the room fills yet again with strange fumes. They can no longer see the Conjuror, though his stern voice can still be heard. Suddenly, the Crackerjack appears, now less mischievous but looking most annoyed.

RUPERT FEELS HAPPY AGAIN

" Look! There he goes," cries Rupert Bear,
" Straight into all that smoke down there! "

" The Conjuror's in the circle, too!
I wonder what he's going to do? "

The imp feels cross—look at his face!
He's helpless, now the lid's in place!

" When you go home again, Ting Ling,
You takee back this naughty thing! "

Rupert and his pals crouch to dodge the darting Crackerjack. Bingo is specially anxious not to have his spectacles snatched again, though he need not worry. The little creature seems to be trying without success to keep away from something. After a few moments it plunges head first into the densest part of the cloud. " Look, I can just see the outline of the Conjuror," says Rupert. " He's right in the middle of the circle now, and listen, I think he's doing something to that glass jar." Gently the latest clouds thin out and lift, revealing the figure of the Conjuror holding up the jar. Its lid is now in place and inside it crouches the Crackerjack still looking exceedingly annoyed. The man sits down and calls Rupert and the others round him. " When you go back to China, Ting Ling, you take Clackerjack and give um to Sorcerer, your master. He make great mistake not keeping Clackerjack under control. Tell him he owe me valuable Ming vase."

RUPERT AND HIS CHUMS TIDY UP

As the Conjuror goes away
He says, " I leave you here to play."

The chums then plan to have some fun
When all the clearing up is done.

Sighs Rupert, " Oh, how glad we are
The Crackerjack is in the jar ! "

They ask Ting Ling to tell them more,
And gather round him on the floor.

Making sure that the lid of the glass jar is firmly fixed the Conjuror solemnly bids them good-bye. " Now enjoy your party," he says, " and no Clackerjack to make mischief or tease any more." Then away he goes. " That all velly well," says Tigerlily, sighing with relief, " but no can have nice party while floor covered with bits. We clean up, yes ? " " Of course we will, we'll all help," Rupert agrees cheerfully. So the pals set to work and the house soon looks shipshape. When all are ready to begin Tigerlily takes Rupert to make sure the Crackerjack is secure. " See, him smiling again ! " she says. " Him know no more mischief possible here, but him no care. Back in China him start plenty, plenty new mischief. Oh dear, me t'ink him velly, velly bad." Now that they can breathe freely once more the pals want to know more about it, so Ting Ling starts the party by telling thrilling and hair-raising tales of the naughty Crackerjacks of China.

AN EASY WAY TO MAKE

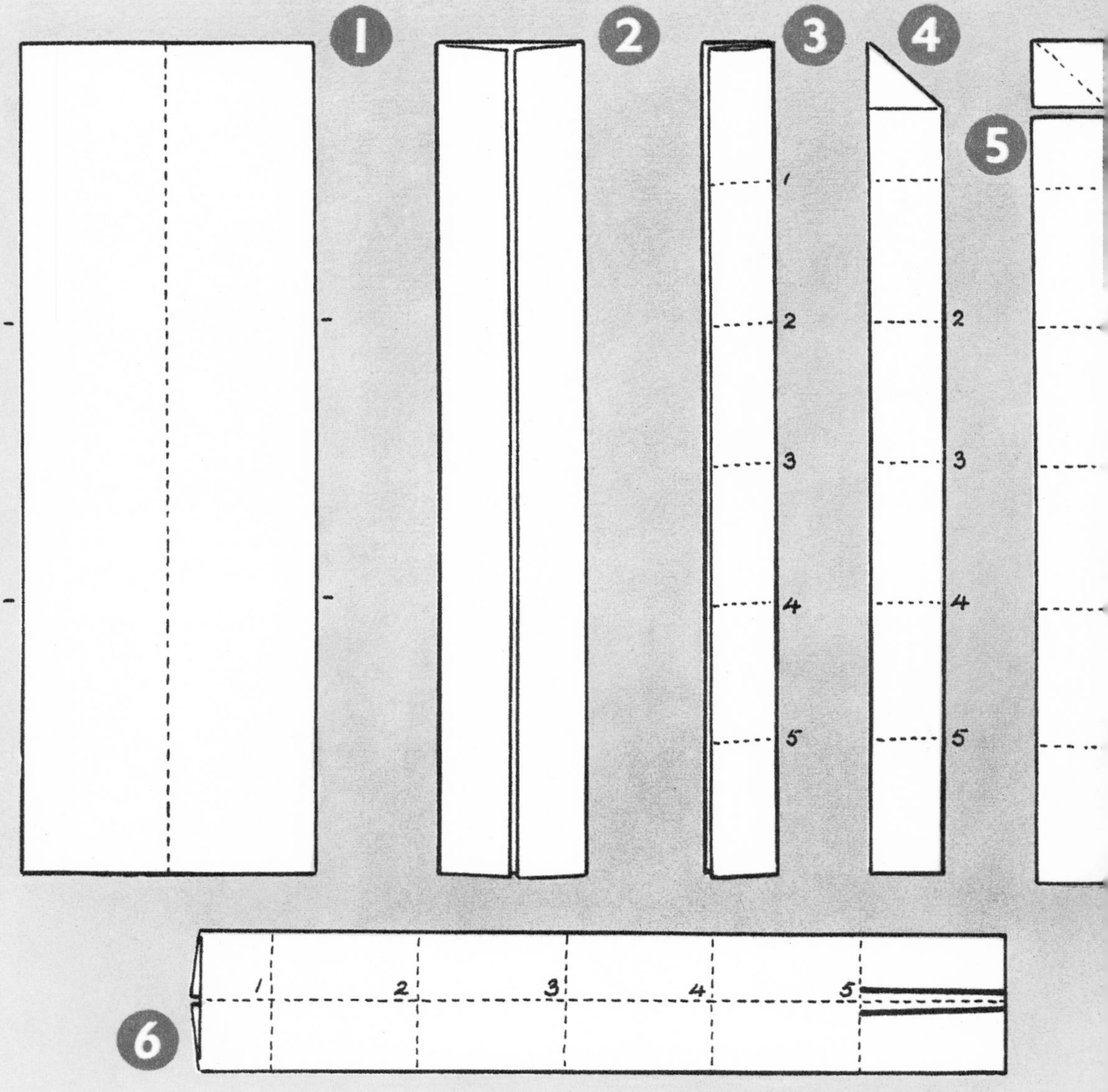

1

2

3

4

5

1

2

3

4

5

2

3

4

5

6

1 2 3 4 5

Your dog will look even jollier with a tiny bow of ribbon tied round his neck.

To make this Scottie dog you need a piece of thin, strong paper three times as long as it is broad. Fold it in half to give the dotted line in Fig. 1. Turn the sides to the middle line (Fig. 2), press flat and fold in half lengthwise (Fig. 3). Mark into six equal parts and number the dividing lines 1 to 5.

Fold down the top corner (Fig. 4), cut off the square you have made (Fig. 5) and throw it away. Next partly open the paper (as in Fig. 2) and make two cuts from the edge through the last section as shown in Fig. 6. Be careful to cut only one thickness of paper. This will be the dog's tail so make it narrower at the end.

Then refold the last two sections but reverse the middle fold for sections

RUPERT'S PAPER SCOTTIE

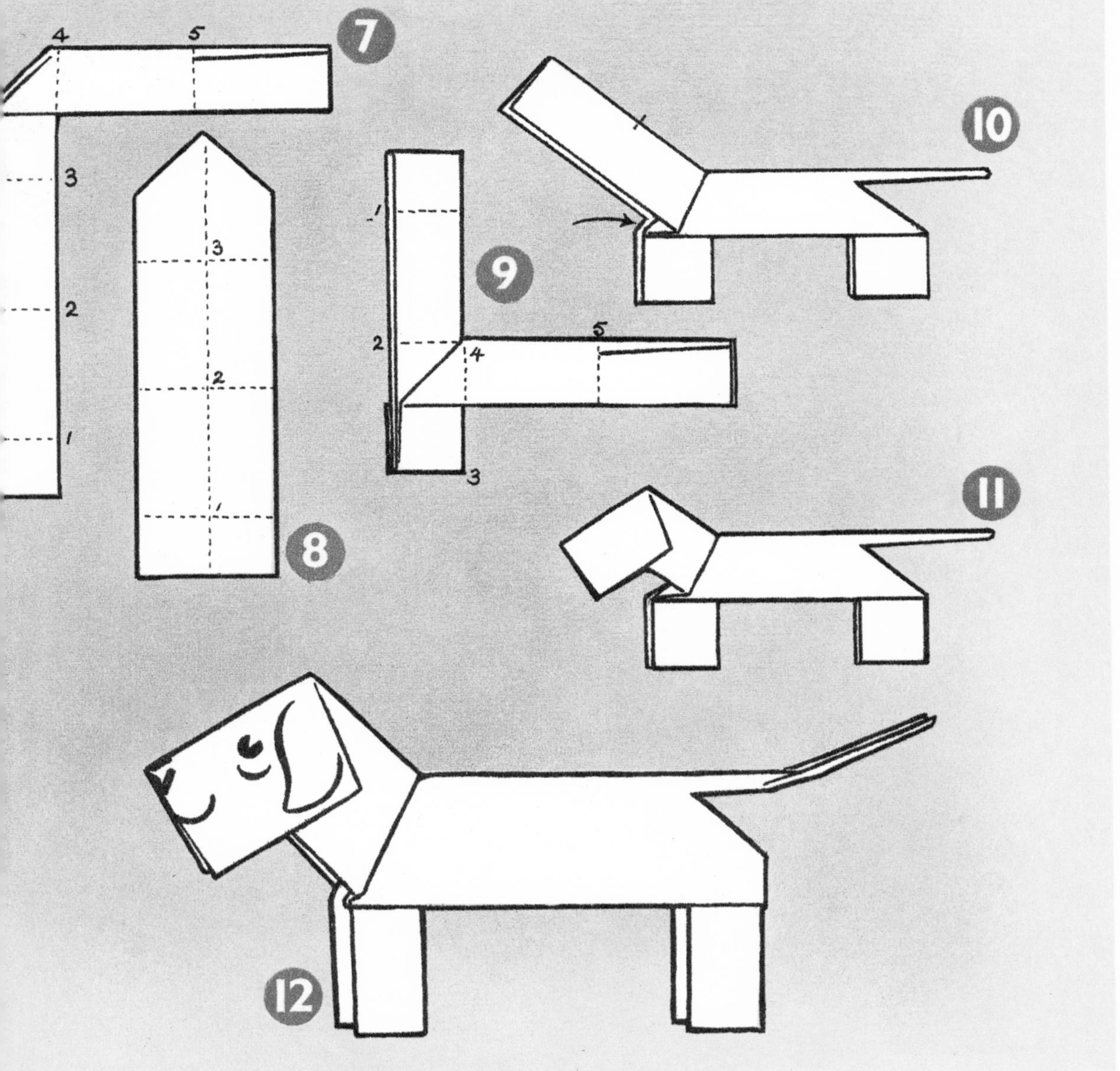

one to four and turn down at right angles to give Fig. 7. Open out sections one to four (Fig. 8), turn up the lower part along division three and close the sides as in Fig. 9.

Now bend the upper part forward, opening slightly so that the resulting folds (arrowed) can be pressed flat (Fig. 10). Also fold the section below the tail inward and downward for the hind legs. Next mark a point rather less than halfway up the sloping edge and bend the top portion forward again, pressing the folds as before (Fig. 11).

Cut the front legs apart. If all the legs look too thick fold part of each one inwards (Fig. 12). Press all folds very firmly. Lastly draw the dog's face.

Another idea is to make a slit at the dog's mouth to hold a bone cut out of paper.

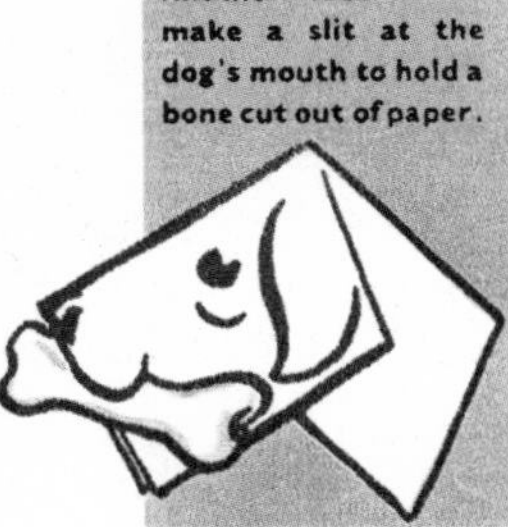

Rupert has an afternoon's holiday from school, so he sets out for his favourite spot in the country, hoping to meet some of his little friends of the fields and woods. It is his lucky day, for he finds some of them gathered on a sandy slope. " Why, there's the rabbit and the robin and the hedgehog," he whispers, edging his way up a grassy bank, " and there's the squirrel too ! " He

looks further and sees a mole and a harvest mouse. " Fancy finding six all at once ! " he thinks. " If I keep very still I can watch them from here." Each circle shows the home of one of the creatures. Can you tell which is which ? Some are easy, but others may make you think hard. Write your list, then turn to the answers on page 107 and see how many you have got right.

Nutwood's lovely trees are in danger, and time is short if they are to be saved. Deep in the pine wood an attack has been planned!

Rupert's mummy says, " My dear,
We'll need some wood, for winter's near."

" It won't take long to fill the sack,"
Says Rupert, " and I'll soon be back."

He hears a cuckoo call nearby,
" It's late," he thinks, " to hear that cry."

The answer soon is plain to see,
Says Beryl, " That call came from me."

SUMMER is passing and Rupert has been looking for the biggest stones he can find in order to build his own rock garden for next year, when Mrs. Bear comes to him. " Colder weather will be here soon," she says. " Would you like to collect some sticks for starting fires ? " " Right-ho," says Rupert cheerfully. " I should think pine twigs and fir cones would be best, if I can find any." And, rolling up the sack that his mother has brought, he trots away towards the forest. Reaching the edge of the trees, Rupert pauses. " Surely that was the call of the cuckoo," he thinks. Next moment he hears a chuckle and the smiling face of Beryl, the Girl Guide, appears over the leaves. " Got you that time, Rupert ! " she laughs. " Yes, I'm afraid you did," says the little bear cheerfully, " but I ought to have known it wasn't a real cuckoo. They've all flown away long ago. I'm looking for fir cones. What are you doing here ? "

RUPERT GETS A CHALLENGE

The three Guides say, " We've just begun
To look for acorns. It's such fun."

Laughs Rupert Bear, " Now off you go.
We'll meet here in an hour or so."

" That pine-tree forest is the spot
For fir cones—you will find a lot."

" It's raining," Rupert says, and he
Trots off to wait beneath a tree.

Guide Beryl leads Rupert to her pals Pauline and Janet who are nearby. They have small sacks about the same size as his own. " We're collecting things too," Beryl says, " we're looking for acorns. We haven't had much luck so far, although there are lots of oak trees about everywhere." " Well, I haven't found any pine trees yet," says Rupert. " But there must be some not far away. Let's meet in about two hours and see who has collected the most." The three Guides like the idea of the competition with Rupert. " There are only a few pine trees in this wood," says Beryl, " it would be fairer if we showed you where you could find some more." So Janet takes him and points across a hill. " There's a whole pine forest over there," she declares. Thanking her, Rupert hurries away. Almost at once there is a shower of rain. " I must shelter for a minute," he murmurs. " There's someone under that big tree. I do believe it's old Gaffer Jarge."

RUPERT SHELTERS AWHILE

He greets the Gaffer with a smile
And waiting there they chat awhile.

The old man says, " Those pines have spread."
And with a sigh he shakes his head.

He adds, " If I could have my way
I'd chop the whole lot down today."

They part and Rupert once again
Sets off amid a fall of rain.

" Well, Gaffer," says Rupert cheerfully, as he reaches the fence. " Are you admiring the view ? " To his astonishment the old man seems very annoyed. " No, I b'aint admiring no view," he growls. " 'Tis nothing but gloomy old pine forests. I mind the time when this was all Nutwood forest as far as the eye can see. Good English trees ; oak and beech and ash and thorn, rowan and ladybirch and the little glades lit with spindle berries ; bluebells in the spring ; and look at it now ! All black pines and naught'll grow with 'em ! " " I'm sorry you don't like the pine trees," says Rupert. " I'm just going to collect twigs and cones for Mummy's winter fires." " Glad to hear it," snorts Gaffer Jarge. " I wish you'd collect the whole pinewood. I've watched it coming nearer every year and it ought to be stopped ! " When the rain ceases he moves away still grumbling. Rupert crosses the valley, and by the time he reaches the trees another shower of rain is falling.

RUPERT BECOMES SCARED

He stoops to gather up a cone
And feels so gloomy all alone.

Then comes a funny rustling sound
And nervously he looks around.

A pine-clad creature startles him,
He steps back, for it looks so grim.

The stranger bounds off out of sight,
And Rupert runs with all his might.

Entering the pine-wood, Rupert starts picking up twigs and cones and putting them into his sack. " Some cones are heavier than others," he thinks. " I'll choose the light ones. They'll burn just as well. What a weird place this is, all gloomy and silent. I don't wonder Gaffer Jarge doesn't like it; I wish I had somebody to talk to." Just then he hears a rustling sound. " Hullo," he murmurs. " There's something here alive beside me. I wonder if it's a rabbit." He moves towards the sound and suddenly he is startled by a hiss near his ear. Spinning round he sees a queer little figure clothed in pine needles standing on a dead branch. " Please, who are you ? " he quavers. But the other doesn't say a word. He only scowls more fiercely before bounding away and disappearing. " Oh dear, this is no place for me," Rupert mutters. His sack is nearly full, so he turns and hurries away, making for the edge of the wood as quickly as he can.

RUPERT FINDS A TINY DOOR

But in his haste he goes astray
And very soon he's lost his way.

He sees a door half hidden by
Enormous boulders, piled up high.

The little bear then stops to read
A tree-bark message, strange indeed !

He turns to find that near at hand
Four scowling little figures stand.

Before he has gone very far, Rupert realises that he has wandered in many different directions, and now he cannot recognise any of the places that he knows. " I don't know which way to go for Nutwood," he thinks. The rain has stopped, but no sunlight comes through the trees, and he cannot see the edge of the wood. Reaching a great pile of boulders he decides to have a rest, and to his amazement he discovers a tiny door underneath the biggest rock. Rupert scrambles to examine the little door which he finds is locked. On the ground he sees a piece of pine bark. " This seems to have been pinned on the door, but it has fallen off," he mutters. " Hullo, there's some faint writing on it. It says ' Final assault. The army assembles at sunset at . . .' Then it fades right out. This is queer. What does it mean ? " It sounds interesting so he pops it into his sack. A moment later there is another noise and he sees four little faces scowling at him.

RUPERT FACES THE OGRE

They gather round and loudly cry :
" So, stranger, you have come to spy."

" You come inside with us," they say,
" And meet our master right away."

The Ogre eyes him with a glare
And asks what he is doing there.

" There shall be none but pine-trees here,
All other kinds shall disappear."

The little prickly men face Rupert fiercely. " We've watched you long enough," says one of them. " What are you doing here ? Who sent you to spy on us ? " " I'm not spying," says Rupert. " I'm only out collecting twigs and fir cones. But, please, who are you and what's this door ? " " Never mind that," says the creature. " Our master, the Pine Ogre, will answer your questions—if he wants to." More little figures appear. They unlock the door, and hustle Rupert through it. He is taken through a short dark passage and is soon facing the tall, forbidding figure of the Pine Ogre. His face is grim, as if he had never smiled. " And what is a stranger doing here ? " he demands. " Oh please, I'm picking up fir cones," says Rupert nervously, " and the Guides are collecting acorns and . . ." " Ha, acorns ! " interrupts the Ogre harshly. " They'd better hurry. Soon there will be no more acorns and no more oak trees. That I have decided."

RUPERT IS SENT AWAY

" As Lord of Silence it's my will
To live in pine woods dark and still."

Then clutching hands seize Rupert Bear
As he calls out, " It isn't fair ! "

The Ogre thunders, " It's too late,
No one can alter Nutwood's fate."

With that he gives a mighty shout,
" Slaves, take this bear and send him out."

Rupert is startled. " How can you do such a thing ? " he asks. " Who are you ? " " They call me the Pine Ogre," says the other sternly. " I am the Lord of Silence. Silence I must have —and what is so silent as a pine wood ? I have determined that Nutwood forest shall be mine. Its trees shall disappear and in their place pines shall grow and I—I shall reign in the midst of them." " But you can't, you mustn't ! " says Rupert. Before he can say any more he is seized and dragged away. Rupert is not taken far before the Pine Ogre recalls him. " Why should we trouble ourselves about a little bear ? " he says, frowning darkly. " It matters not that he knows our plans. He is weak and it is too late for him to do anything to hinder us. Show him the way home and forbid him to come back. Now I must return to my silence." His little slaves take Rupert again and hustle him away down the little path to the small door by which he first entered.

RUPERT GOES ON ALONE

The Ogre's slaves take Rupert back
To where he left his firewood sack.

A frowning slave says, " Now make haste,
I've very little time to waste."

Then Rupert loses sight of him
As they approach the forest rim.

So Rupert makes for open ground,
And sees the Gaffer homeward bound.

Rupert is glad to be back in the open air and he bends down to pick up his sack of fir cones. " Phew, I had no idea there was anyone like that in the pine wood," he murmurs. " What a terrible person." " Don't call him names," snaps one of the little creatures severely. " You wouldn't know he was here if you hadn't accidently found this door. Now hurry. I've been told to show you the way home." And he leads Rupert rapidly away without saying another word. The little bear has to run fast to keep his leader in sight. At length the prickly little creature dodges behind a tree and disappears. " What is he up to now ? " murmurs Rupert. Then he realises that he has been brought to the edge of the wood and can see daylight through the trees. Thankfully he hurries out and runs across the valley. " Gaffer Jarge ought to hear about this," he thinks anxiously as he reaches the fence. Peering down the slope he sees the old man trudging homewards to his cottage.

RUPERT TELLS THE GUIDES

He runs to tell the aged man
About the Ogre's wicked plan.

But Gaffer scoffs, " A likely tale ! "
And hobbles off to Nutwood Vale.

" *I'll tell the Guides, that's what I'll do,*"
Thinks Rupert. " *They will know it's true.*"

But very doubtful, too, they seem.
They think that Rupert's had a dream !

" I say, Gaffer," Rupert calls out breathlessly. " I've been in the pine-wood and you were quite right. It is spreading this way. It's the work of the Pine Ogre, and he says that he's going to destroy all the rest of the trees in Nutwood forest and have only pines there, too, and . . . " But Gaffer Jarge gives a grunt. " Hey, hey ! I'm too old for your fairy tales, young Rupert," he wheezes. " Pine Ogres, what nonsense ! " and he walks away. When Gaffer Jarge has gone Rupert remembers the three Guides and his arrangement to meet them in two hours. Hurrying to the woods, he finds them waiting for him. " You have been a long time," says Pauline. " Did you find all you wanted ? " Rupert pours out his strange story of the Pine Ogre, but the Guides only smile mischievously. " Oh, Rupert, surely that's a dream ! " says Beryl. " Anyway you've won the competition. I can see that your sack's full. We've had no luck with the acorns."

Rupert and the Pine Ogre

RUPERT CLIMBS AN OAK TREE

The Guides have searched around, and yet
They found the acorns hard to get.

They wander off and all look vexed,
While Rupert hesitates, perplexed.

" Ah," Rupert says, " I think it's clear
Why acorns are so scarce this year."

He sees a squirrel on a bough,
And asks, " Where are the acorns now ? "

Rupert insists that his adventure was not a dream, and the Girl Guides begin to look worried. " It would be awful if it were true," says Beryl. " We don't want to lose our beautiful forest and have only pine trees. And things *are* rather queer here. Thousands of acorns have fallen, but there's hardly one on the ground ! Do you think the Pine Ogre has taken them to prevent any more oak trees growing ? " They resume their search and Rupert stands pondering over what he has heard. " If all the acorns are disappearing it must be part of the Ogre's work," he muses, " though he sounds as though he meant to destroy the wood more quickly than that." Then a bright idea strikes him. " Why, of course, I know who may have taken them," he chuckles. Choosing a tree that is easy to climb he soon discovers a squirrel. " Hi, have you and all your pals been taking the acorns ? " he calls. The squirrel looks at Rupert. " What makes you ask that ? " it demands.

RUPERT FOLLOWS A SQUIRREL

The squirrel gasps to hear the news
That in the forest danger brews.

He sets off at a flying pace,
And through the woodland ways they race.

Then gleaming in the sunshine bright,
Some tumbling waters come in sight.

Beside the rocks, the squirrel stops
And in a cleft a stone he drops.

"Something very strange is happening to the acorns this year," continues the squirrel, "but how should you know anything about it ?" When the little bear tells him of what has happened and of the Pine Ogre's threat, the squirrel gets very excited. "This is important, very important !" it squeaks. "We must get help. Follow me." So Rupert descends, picks up his sack and tries to keep the squirrel in sight as it leaps along through the branches. Reaching a rougher part of the wood, the squirrel leaves the branches and runs uphill over rocks and grassy tufts so fast that Rupert can hardly keep pace. At length the creature pauses at the edge of a lovely little waterfall. "Who *are* you searching for ?" asks Rupert breathlessly. "Don't talk," says the squirrel sharply. "The water's already making too much noise and I must listen." Darting around, it drops a small pebble into a narrow cleft between two large boulders.

RUPERT TALKS TO AN ELF

*It falls as though inside a well,
And makes a sound clear as a bell.*

*They wait nearby the waterfall
And presently they hear a call.*

*An elfin figure says, " Now pray,
What is that you wish to say ? "*

*" I cannot stop here long with you,"
He cries, " I've lots of work to do."*

Above the roar of the waterfall the pebble goes clattering down in the darkness, and to Rupert's surprise there is a tiny tinkling sound as if it has hit a bell. " Now we must wait," says the squirrel, as it hops away to a rock near the water. " There's no knowing where he may appear." " Where who may appear ? " asks Rupert. " Is it . . . ? " But before he can say any more there is a sudden noise behind them that makes them both jump. Swinging round, Rupert and the squirrel find themselves facing a small frowning figure in a spiky hat. " Who are you two ? " he says sharply. " Why have you summoned me ? " " Please, I did it," says the squirrel. " I'm terribly worried ; something awfully queer is happening in the forest. All the acorns are disappearing as soon as they fall and . . ." " D'you think I don't know that ? " exclaims the other. " We are more worried than you are, so don't waste any more of my time. I must be off."

RUPERT HAS IMPORTANT NEWS

Says Rupert, " You're an Autumn Elf,
I've got some news for you myself."

The elf says, " I've no time to spare,
I know there's mischief in the air."

" Please listen," Rupert begs, " you'll find
I know what's in the Ogre's mind."

At Rupert's words the elf turns back,
" Do you know when he will attack ? "

Rupert has been staring at the little stranger. " I say, I know you, don't I ? " he says at last. " Surely you're one of the Autumn Elves. I've got something to tell you too." " Some other time," says the elf. " I can't wait now. We're too busy trying to check the trouble that the Pine Ogre is causing." He hurries away, but Rupert runs after him. " Hi, don't go," he shouts urgently. " That's what I want to talk to you about. I've just come from the pine forest and I've seen him ! " The Autumn Elf is in a hurry, but at Rupert's words he stops abruptly. " What's that you say ? You've seen the Pine Ogre ! You can't have. He is too well guarded." " Yes, I did ! " insists Rupert. " His little slaves caught me and took me to him, and then let me go. I think he's horrid ; he's going to turn all this forest into a pine wood very soon." " But how soon ? " cries the elf in great excitement. " We must know that or we shall be lost ! "

RUPERT HUNTS WITH PAULINE

Guide Pauline pops up, keen to see
Who Rupert's little friends can be.

But frightened by a stranger's face
The elf has vanished without trace.

" Let's call him," Pauline says. They shout
And both look hopefully about.

Cries Rupert Bear, " You can depend
On Girl Guide Pauline—she's a friend."

Before Rupert can answer, Pauline the Girl Guide appears behind him. " I heard your voice, and came to see who you were talking to," she says. " Who was it ? " The squirrel and the elf have leaped away and Rupert can see nothing of them. " We were talking of the Pine Ogre and the disappearing acorns," he says. " The Autumn Elf might be able to do something about it, but you've frightened him away. We must get him back somehow." Rupert and Pauline call again and again, and search near the waterfall, and at length the squirrel leads the elf back to them. They look at the Guide very suspiciously. " I'm not supposed to show myself to humans," says the elf frowning. " Who are you ? " " Oh please, don't be afraid," says Rupert. " Pauline is a friend, and she's worried about the acorns, too." " Then let's get down to business," says the elf. " If we are not going to lose our forest we must discover the Pine Ogre's plans."

RUPERT EMPTIES HIS SACK

The Autumn Elf says, " We must beat
The Ogre's army when we meet."

" In that case," Rupert says, " my clue
May prove quite valuable to you."

" That piece of bark will tell you all
Although the writing's very small."

The elf then shouts, " Is this a prank ?
Where are the words—the bark is blank ! "

Pauline is thrilled to learn that Rupert's story of the Pine Ogre is not a fairy tale, and the elf is soon talking to her freely. " Our trouble is that we elves are too busy to be always on the look-out for the Ogre's slaves," he says. " They go around in a sort of army, and if we knew their plans we could get together and meet them, and stop them spoiling our forest." Suddenly Rupert jumps up. " Did you say an army ? " he asks. " I believe I can help you there ! " What Rupert has remembered is the piece of bark he picked up in the pine forest. Running to his sack he tips out some of the cones. Sure enough, the bark is there and, picking it up, he hands it to the Autumn Elf. " There's a message on it—something about an army assembling," he says. The elf looks at it. Then he turns it over and frowns. " I don't know what you're talking about," he grumbles. " There's no writing at all on this ! " " But—but I read it myself not long ago," falters Rupert.

RUPERT'S CLUE IS USEFUL

But Pauline says : " This is, I think
All written in a special ink."

" Just wait," she adds, " and do not fret.
The words may show when this is wet."

So carefully she soaks the bark
And hopes to show up every mark.

The Autumn Elf then gives a cheer,
For now the writing's very clear.

Rupert is bewildered by the mystery of the piece of bark. " Are you sure that there was a message on this ? " asks Pauline as she takes it. " Of course I am," says the little bear. Then the Guide asks a curious question. " What sort of weather was it when you found this ? " " Let me see, it had just stopped raining," says Rupert. Pauline smiles. " I believe that the words are written in some sort of invisible ink that only shows when it is wet," she declares. "Now the bark is dry and it has vanished." Rupert is full of excitement at the Guide's idea for solving the mystery, and the party moves towards the waterfall. There Pauline holds the bark under the spray until it is wet. Then she hands it to the Autumn Elf. " You're right, you're right ! " he cries. " The writing is quite clear now. Listen, this is what it says : ' Final assault. The army assembles at sunset at the withered oak.' Good gracious, that means that we have no time to lose."

RUPERT HAS A WARNING

" The message tells just when and where
The pine slaves meet—we must *be there ! "*

He leads them to a withered tree,
" That is the Ogre's work," says he.

He warns the chums, " Now keep away
From this place at the close of day."

With that, before their very eyes
He disappears. " Oh ! " Pauline cries.

Rupert still can't understand the full meaning of the message, but the Autumn Elf leaps away in the greatest of glee. " Come, I'll show you," he says, pointing to where a large oak stands black and withered and stripped of its leaves. " That only happened a few days ago and it's the Ogre's doing. Now that we know his slaves are gathering there I can bring my brother elves and we can meet them and we'll whack them. Despite all their wicked ways, the Nutwood forest shall not become a pine-wood ! " The Autumn Elf becomes more and more brisk. " You people had better keep well away from here at sunset," he declares. " All sorts of things may be happening and it won't be safe." Then he turns and in a moment has disappeared. " Well, what a queer affair ! " gasps Pauline. " Beryl and Janet will never believe it when I tell them." " Yes, it has been an odd adventure," agrees Rupert. So they separate and he goes to find his sack of fir cones.

RUPERT FETCHES THE GAFFER

Then carrying his fir-cone store
The little bear goes home once more.

Though tea is laid, he's very keen
To tell the Gaffer where he's been.

" Now Gaffer, I will prove to you
That what I said was really true."

Old Gaffer plods on with his stick.
He hopes it's not another trick !

When Pauline and the squirrel have gone their different ways, Rupert makes for home with his sack of fir cones. Mrs. Bear meets him and, to her surprise, Rupert is eager to go straight out again. " I've had such an adventure," he says. " And it isn't finished. May I go back and tell Gaffer Jarge and see what the elves will do at sunset by the withered oak ? " Mrs. Bear stares. " I've no idea what you're talking about," she says. " You haven't had your tea yet, but if it's so important, you may go. Come back before dark." Leaving his home Rupert hurries to find Gaffer Jarge. " I say, Gaffer," he calls. " You remember what you were saying about the pine forest creeping nearer ? Well, I've found out all that's happening. I've seen the Pine Ogre and wonderful things are going to happen at the withered oak. Do come, it's not far." " Well, if you're playing a trick it'll be the worse for you," wheezes Gaffer as he rises and hobbles off with the little bear.

Rupert and the Pine Ogre

RUPERT SEES A VICTORY

*And Pauline too is there to see
The battle round the old oak tree.*

*The Ogre's men, in sorry plight,
Give in with very little fight.*

*" Oh, Jarge," says Rupert. " This is grand."
But Gaffer cannot understand.*

*The elf says, " There, we've won the day
And saved the Nutwood trees ! Hooray ! "*

At the top of the slope, Rupert spies the Guide Pauline waiting. " I just had to see what happens at sunset," she whispers, " and it's nearly time now." They all crouch in the bushes and watch. Presently a long line of tiny prickly figures appear moving towards Nutwood forest. Hardly have they reached the withered oak when hundreds of elves leap out from all sides. In the battle that follows all the Ogre's slaves are surrounded and captured and marched away. For a time Gaffer Jarge stares at Rupert. Then, quite unable to speak, he turns and moves away, shaking his head in bewilderment. But the first elf has spotted the chums and he leaps towards them. " We've won, we've won ! " he cries. " Nutwood forest is saved ! Now we can do our job properly and see that every kind of tree has a proper place. But for you, little bear, pine-woods would have conquered us and now they never will ! " Then he vanishes and Rupert scampers happily home again.

A piece of card is coloured green and cut in eighteen squares, each large enough to cov the head of an imp. Place the cards on the im in the six pine trees (outlined in black) so th only the imps in the Nutwood trees (outlin in red) can be seen. The game is now ready f two persons, who play against each other wi nine pieces of card on facing pages. The id of the game is to drive all the imps from t

utwood trees to the pines. To do this each ayer in turn hides a small button in one hand. the other player guesses the correct hand he ay move one of his cards to a Nutwood tree d cover an imp with it. As the game goes more and more imps in the Nutwood trees ll be covered until the only imps to be seen ll be those in the pine trees. The first ayer to move all his nine cards is the winner.

RUPERT'S FUNFAIR PUZZLE

Rupert and Algy are enjoying all the fun of the fair. "Oh, look! There's a circus," says Algy suddenly, "We simply must not miss that!" So they hurry to the huge tent, and there they meet two clowns. "Please, when does the circus start?" asks Rupert. "Not yet, I'm afraid," sighs Peeko the clown. "Some of our performing animals have strayed away, and we must find them for the next show." Luckily the animals are not far off and if you look carefully you will see them hidden in the picture. When you think you have found them all, check your animals with the answers on page 107.

How to Make

PEEKO THE CLOWN

First trace his body, arms and legs. An easy way is to place a piece of thin card under this page, then draw firmly with your pencil over Peeko's black outlines. This will mark the card clearly enough to guide you when cutting it. Next colour the pieces of card and bore small holes where shown. Join the body, arms and legs with short pieces of thin string and tie knots at the joints so that the arms and legs swing freely. Pass a length of string through the holes in Peeko's hands, putting in the paper tube as shown, and tie the ends of the string together.

MAKE A SMALL TUBE BY ROLLING A NARROW PAPER STRIP. GLUE THE TOP LAYER OF THE STRIP SO THAT THE TUBE WILL NOT UNROLL.

How to work your toy

Cross the strings and stretch the loops between your fingers and thumbs. Each time you jerk the strings Peeko will swing over and over.

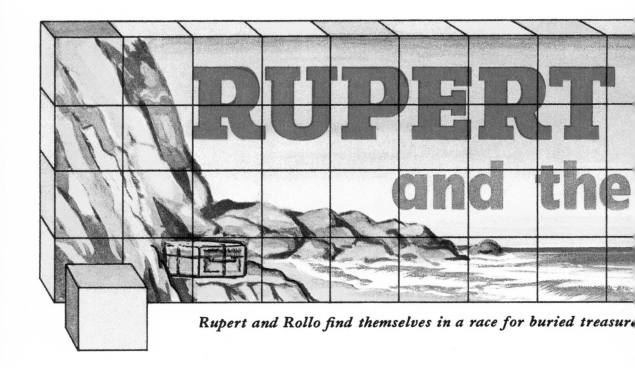

RUPERT and the

Rupert and Rollo find themselves in a race for buried treasur

One summer day while Rupert's out,
He hears young Rollo give a shout.

Across the grass a stranger comes
And hurriedly makes for the chums.

ONE warm summer day, Rupert goes to Nutwood Common to see if he can find any blackberries, " I wish I had remembered to bring a basket," he murmurs, " I could have taken back enough for Mummy to make a blackberry tart." But when Rupert finds some of the berries and tastes them he gives a shiver. " They *are* sour ! " he says, " they aren't ripe enough yet. I had better come back later." He is about to turn homeward when he hears a cheery call and sees his friend Rollo, the gipsy boy. " Hullo, hullo ! " calls out Rupert, stopping for his chum. " If you are looking for blackberries, it is too early for them." Rollo grins and shakes his head. " I have been too busy to go blackberrying," he replies, " and you are just the person I want, Rupert. Are you fond of mysteries ? " The little bear nods. " Oo-oo ! Rather ! Why ? Have you found something mysterious ?" " I think so," replies Rollo, "there is something strange going on – "

LION ROCK

which takes them to an island far across the sea

The stranger stops and gasps, " I say,
Does Sailor Sam live round this way ? "

" Why," Rupert says, " I'll show you where
To find Sam's shack—it's over there."

" Hi, there ! " A sudden shout interrupts Rollo, and the chums turn to see a bearded gentleman running towards them. " Who is he ? " whispers Rupert. " I have never seen him before." The man is panting hard as he reaches the chums and mops his brow. " I hope you two can help me," he says. " I am looking for a fellow named Sailor Sam. I want to find him quickly—there is no time to lose. Do either of you know him ? " " Why, yes sir," says Rupert at once. " He is an old friend of mine. He lives in a little shack on top of this hill. If you want to get there quickly you had better let me show you the way." " Splendid ! " says the stranger. " It is lucky I met you or I might have spent hours searching by myself." Rupert is longing to hear more of Rollo's mystery and he asks the gipsy boy to wait. " I will come back as soon as I have taken this gentleman to Sailor Sam," he says. " Don't go away, Rollo." Then Rupert leads the stranger farther up the hill.

RUPERT KNOWS WHERE TO GO

So Rupert leads the way until
He sees Sam working on the hill.

Old Sam is taken by surprise.
" My skipper ! Welcome, sir ! " he cries.

The skipper makes sure no one's near
To spy on him and overhear.

The little bear then turns away,
But Sam's old skipper bids him stay.

The way to Sailor Sam's shack is mostly uphill and Rupert goes on ahead until he catches sight of his friend. " Hi, Sam," he calls. " I've brought someone to see you and he's in a hurry." Looking puzzled, the sailor walks to meet the stranger and gazes at him for a moment. Then he gives a glad shout. " Why, if it isn't my old skipper ! I heard you'd become an admiral, sir. And have you come to see Sailor Sam ? This is, indeed, a great day for me ! " The old admiral smiles at Sailor Sam's welcome. Then he gazes round to make sure no one else is in earshot before he says, " I'm glad I've found you, Sam. Are you prepared to come on a secret voyage with me ? " " Aye, aye, sir, anywhere in the world ! " cries the sailor happily. " Come into my shack. We can't be overheard there." Thinking his work is finished, Rupert moves away, but the admiral calls to him. " There's going to be a shower. You'd better come inside too. I'm sure our secret will be safe with you."

Rupert and the Lion Rock

RUPERT HEARS A SECRET

The paper, so the sailor hears,
Was hidden for a hundred years.

But Sam says, " Sir, I can't make out
What this strange writing's all about."

" The hiding place is on this chart,"
The skipper says. " When can we start ? "

He needs help on his treasure cruise
And tells Sam there's no time to lose.

Feeling very proud to be trusted with a secret, Rupert goes into the shack with the two men. The admiral takes from his pocket an old, faded sheet which he unfolds and lays on the table. " There, Sam," he says, " that is my great secret. It had been hidden in my house for over a hundred years and no-one knew where it was. At last my handyman and I found it behind a panel. It tells where a lot of my family fortune is hidden." Rupert is as puzzled as Sailor Sam by the strange marks on the old chart and the admiral smiles. " It is, of course, in code," he says. " My handyman and I worked very hard until we solved it. We found that the treasure is buried by the tree under Lion Rock on Nicholas Island. My ancestor, who buried the treasure named the island after him. And now, Sam, there's no time to lose. We need a small boat and we need another man." " Can't we take your handyman, sir ? " says Sam. " The man who has helped you already."

RUPERT IS DISAPPOINTED

" My handyman's gone off, and so
He means to get there first, I know."

" Then sir," says Sam, " let's hurry, do."
And Rupert asks, " May I come too ? "

Alas, the skipper can't agree
For Rupert Bear to cross the sea.

So Rupert leaves and gives his word,
To tell nobody what he's heard.

At Sam's suggestion the admiral looks grim. " I naturally thought my handyman would come with me," he says. " He's the only other person who knows my secret. But a week ago he disappeared and no one has seen him since. You can guess what's in my mind." " Gracious, then we've no time to lose," says Sam. " I can get just the boat you need, sir, and I'll bring Cornish Jake. He's trustworthy and we can start in two days." " Oh, do let me come too," begs Rupert, and the two men look amused at his excitement. The rain has stopped, so they all move outside where he goes on pleading. " And what could a little bear do on such a journey ? " smiles the admiral. " No, no, it may be very dangerous and you're too small. Meanwhile, promise that you won't tell a soul what you've heard." Rupert promises at once, but he is very disappointed. Leaving the others to continue their plans, he walks home. " If only I could go," he sighs.

RUPERT AND ROLLO FIND A SHIP

Exciting news makes Rupert keen
To know just what his friend has seen.

Towards the trees the gipsy goes
Without a sound as he tip-toes.

They reach the woods and look around,
Says Rollo, " Hush, don't make a sound."

Down to the river creep the pair
And find a ship is hidden there.

Having made his promise to keep the admiral's secret, Rupert is anxious lest Rollo should ask questions. However, when he rejoins his friend, he finds him full of his own affairs. " Now, then, would you like to solve my mystery ? " says Rollo. " Why, yes, of course," says Rupert. " What is it ? " " It's down in that thick clump of willows," replies the boy. " You know the place where the river spreads into a wide, deep pool ? But come, I'll show you." And, jumping up, he leads the way rapidly downhill. As he reaches the lower woods, Rollo goes cautiously. Telling Rupert to be very quiet, he stops and listens and keeps a sharp look-out. At length they reach the willows and, lying down, they crawl near to the water's edge. Across the wide pool Rupert can see a vessel partly hidden by more willows. " What ship is that ? " he whispers. " That's what I want to know," breathes Rollo. " I've seen the men on it and they're a queer lot."

Rupert and the Lion Rock

RUPERT GOES ON BOARD

Across the little bridge they creep
And Rollo takes a cautious peep.

The ship is empty, there's no doubt.
" But why ? " says Rollo, " Let's find out."

Then by the handrail Rupert waits,
While on deck Rollo hesitates.

All's clear, they find, and then they go
To search a cabin down below.

Rupert and Rollo wait and watch in silence. There's no sound from the mystery vessel, and at length the gipsy boy sits up. " I don't believe any of the men are on board," he whispers. " Let's try and look into this more closely." Moving cautiously upstream he finds a bridge and, crossing it, he leads the way down the other bank until they can push through the thick grass to the ship. They creep towards it, still listening for the strangers. After a long pause, Rollo screws up his courage, climbs slowly over the rail and steps gently on to the deck. The ship dips and sways very slightly on the current, but nothing else happens. Rupert follows as the boy goes quietly down below to explore. " Those men are certainly living here," murmurs Rollo, " but who are they ? Why have they come ? " " I don't yet see why you are so suspicious of them," says Rupert. " Just wait until you see them," answers Rollo. " Then you'll be suspicious, too ! "

RUPERT HIDES FROM THE MEN

Back on the deck, to their dismay,
Strange-looking men are in their way.

" Downstairs, come quick," says Rollo. "Hide ! "
They find a store and creep inside.

Says Rollo, listening at the door,
" There's someone outside, I feel sure."

Two baskets in the store are rammed
And then the little doors are slammed.

After seeing the cabin, Rupert says that they must go back. " We've really no business here at all," he declares. They reach the deck and pause in anxiety. The sound of voices comes from the bank. Peeping round the corner, Rollo sees some men shouldering their way through the willows and he hurriedly draws back. Hardly knowing what they are doing, the two pals tiptoe down below to find somewhere to hide. " Look, there's a dark cupboard," whispers the boy. " In with you, quickly ! " Shutting the little doors after them, the two friends crouch and listen. The space around them is filled with cordage, big bundles and rope fenders all thrown about in confusion. " What a mess ! " murmurs Rollo. " It's just what I expected. I don't believe these men are sailors at all ! " " Hush ! " whispers Rupert, " someone's coming ! " They crawl out of sight just as two wicker baskets are thrust in. Then the doors are slammed and barred.

RUPERT AND ROLLO ARE FOUND

There's no escape, the doors are locked,
No wonder both the chums feel shocked.

They both begin to bang and shout
And hope the men will let them out.

A scowling man flings back the door,
" Please," Rupert gasps, " put us ashore."

The man treats them as stowaways,
" Look, cap'n, at these brats," he says.

Rupert and Rollo gaze around in great anxiety. " We're shut in ! How ever are we going to get away ? " says the little bear. As they crawl round they see that there is no other door. Suddenly there is a noise and the ship trembles as it starts to move. " I hope they won't go far ! " whispers Rollo. But the ship doesn't stop and, at length, it begins to rock. " Gracious, we're going to sea ! We must let them know we're here ! " he says. So they both shout at the top of their voices and bang on the roof. The noise soon attracts attention. The little doors are opened, some bundles are dragged out and next minute Rupert is facing a rough, scowling man. " Please can you put us ashore ? " says Rollo. " Huh, so you're stowaways, are you ? " shouts the man. " Come on out. You'll find you've chosen the wrong boat for that game. We're not turning back for you." And grabbing them both he drags them away and up to the man at the wheel.

RUPERT IS MADE TO WORK

A third man comes. " What's this ? " growls he.
" We'd better throw them in the sea."

The sailor puts the chums to work.
" And see," he grunts, " that you don't shirk."

While Rollo's busy mopping down,
The rough men's plotting makes him frown.

" Those men aren't sailors," he declares,
And then the chums are sent downstairs.

Hearing voices, a third man joins them. The men all glare angrily at the pals. " I found them stowed away below. What shall we do with them ? " says the first man. " Let's throw them overboard," growls another. " Oh please, don't hurt Rupert," says Rollo. " It's my fault we're here." " Never mind all that," says the skipper. " We'll keep them as long as they're useful to us. After that they shall pay the penalty of coming where they're not wanted." Then the pals are hustled away and set to work. The two friends do the jobs they are given and wonder if they will ever see their homes again. Rollo is on the deck when he hears a strange conversation between two of the men and he frowns in a puzzled way. When they are free, he starts to tell Rupert. " I'm certain they're not real sailors," he declares, " but who are they ? " He gets no further before the third man bustles up. " Get below," he snarls. " You can sleep where we found you."

RUPERT KEEPS HIS PROMISE

" Rupert," Rollo says, " I've found
That for the Lion Rock we're bound ! "

" Oh," Rupert gasps, " is that their plan ?
Then one must be the admiral's man."

" I mustn't tell you more," says he.
" But please do help and trust in me."

The days go by, they sail for miles.
And see at last some rocky isles.

Before settling down to sleep Rollo tells Rupert what he has heard. " We're in an awful jam," he sighs. " I heard the skipper say that they wouldn't keep us after they'd reached a place called the Lion Rock and . . ." But Rupert has roused himself with a jerk. " Lion Rock ! " he gasps. " So that's where they are going ! I wonder if one of them is the admiral's handyman." Rollo stares. " What do you mean ? " he demands. " Have you discovered something ? Do tell me." He waits in excitement to know what Rupert's strange words mean, but the little bear pauses and looks thoughtful. " Yes," he says at length, " I think I know what those bad men are after, and who one of them is, but I promised I would tell nobody, so will you trust me and help me to stop them if we can ? " " Why, of course I will," declares Rollo. " But what a thrilling mystery. I wish I knew more about it." So for several days they do their work until some islands appear.

RUPERT STAYS WITH ROLLO

The ship is anchored off the shore
In preparation to explore.

The third man says, " Huh, I'll come too,
I want to keep an eye on you."

The captain scowls, " Don't think you're free,
I'll keep you hard at work, you'll see."

Says Rollo, " This is all so queer,
But Rupert, you must lead, that's clear."

Soon the vessel comes to a standstill and drops anchor in the lee of a rocky reef running out from the largest of the islands. The skipper orders one of the men to lower a boat and row him to the shore. The third man immediately joins them, declaring firmly that he is not going to be left behind, and that he is going to keep an eye on the others. " Good," whispers Rupert. " If they all go there will be no one to keep an eye on us. Perhaps I can think of a plan yet." Before going ashore the skipper frowns at the two pals and tells them to prepare a meal by the time he returns. Then they watch while the men start off from the reef towards the landing beach. " This must be Nicholas Island," murmurs Rupert. " I say, what a lot you know about this queer business," exclaims Rollo. " I just can't make head or tail of it. Anyway, it means that you are the leader now. If you have any plan, just tell me what you want me to do. I'm ready to help."

RUPERT PREPARES THE ROPES

The little bear explains his plan
To foil those rascals, if he can.

First in their sleeping place they grope,
And bring out several coils of rope.

One piece is tied round Rollo's waist,
Another round a pole is placed.

And Rollo says, " Now, little bear,
I'll swim, and you can come by air."

Rupert looks gratefully at his pal. " It's topping of you not to ask me any questions," he says. " All I can say now is that Lion Rock must be on this island. D'you think there is any chance of us getting there before those men ? " " There shall be a way if that's what you want," says Rollo. " Anyway, we certainly won't stay here and prepare a meal for them." Hurrying to their sleeping place, he drags out great lengths of rope of different thicknesses. Rupert helps to lift the cordage from below and spread it on the deck. Rollo ties one end of the thinner cord round his waist. Then, taking the thicker cord, he passes it round the iron support of the flag pole at the stern, and knots the two ends together very firmly. Lastly he ties the other end of the thick cord to the knot. " There, that should do the trick," he says. " I expect I swim better than you, little bear, so I'll get to the rocks by water, and you can come ashore later on by air ! "

Rupert and the Lion Rock

RUPERT'S CHUM SWIMS ASHORE

He dives and Rupert sees him go
Headfirst into the sea below.

With steady strokes he reaches land,
It's Rupert's turn to give a hand.

The rope is paid out length by length
While Rollo hauls with all his strength.

The gipsy boy is satisfied
The rope is strong and firmly tied.

Rupert cannot understand what Rollo means, but he watches while the boy takes off his shirt, scarf and shoes, and ties them into a neat little bundle. Then, after telling Rupert what he means to do, he crawls under the lowest wire, stands for a moment outside the rail, and, with the thin cord still fastened round his waist, he plunges into the sea. Rupert watches admiringly while he strikes out strongly, reaches the rocks, clambers up them, and waves cheerfully from the top. When Rollo has climbed to a suitable spot, he drags on the thin cord, which in turn drags the rope from the ship, while Rupert pays it out so that it passes smoothly on either side of the flag pole. When it is all out, Rollo hauls steadily and firmly. Slowly the vessel swings towards him, and he tugs until the anchor at the prow prevents it moving any further. Lastly, he winds the end of the rope round and round a spur of rock. " That's made it nearly taut," he murmurs. " That's fine."

RUPERT HAS A TRIP BY AIR

Next to the cable Rupert clings
And slowly to the rocks he swings.

He finds the effort such a strain,
He's glad to reach the shore again.

Says Rupert, " Pull the rope ashore,
We may have need of it once more."

" We'd better keep a sharp look-out
In case those rough men are about."

When all is ready, Rupert ties Rollo's bundle firmly round his waist and gets over the rail. Then, gripping the rope, he hangs upside down, and makes his way slowly but surely along. " This must be what Rollo meant when he said that I could reach the rocks by air," he thinks. " It's working splendidly. I'm glad those men can't see us." It is tiring work, but at last he feels himself held by his friend, and he is safely ashore again. A little out of breath after his strange trip, he sits quietly while Rollo puts on his other clothes. " Luckily it's hot on this island," says the gipsy boy. "The sun has almost dried me already." Then, untying the knot, they haul on the end of the rope until it is all ashore. " Now to find the Lion Rock," says Rupert. " Let's bring the ropes with us. We may find them useful later on." They make their way along the broken ridge of the rocks which leads towards the main island. "Keep well down," says Rollo.

RUPERT REACHES LION ROCK

" Ah, here's their boat," he says, " and look !
Those footprints show the way they took."

Their way past trees and shrubs they thread,
To find at last the Lion's head.

Says Rupert, " That's the rock all right.
Let's hurry, it will soon be night."

" And see ! " he cries. " The tree's there too.
So are those men—what will they do ? "

Creeping along, Rupert and Rollo reach a small sandy bay. " There's the men's boat," whispers Rupert, " and look, here are their footmarks. They've gone inland. I wonder if we can get to the place before them ! " " I wish I knew what you were after," sighs Rollo. " However, lead on." So the little bear, not knowing which way to go, turns to the left. After much scrambling and rough going, he pauses. " That great rock ahead," he gasps. " D'you see its shape ? It's just like a lion ! " Rupert feels sure he has found the Lion Rock, but the shades of evening are falling before he and Rollo can get near it. " Yes, look, there's the tree below the rock," Rupert murmurs, " but, oh dear, those men have reached it first ! " " Do tell me how you knew there'd be a tree there and what this is all about," pleads Rollo. " I can't, not yet," says Rupert. " I promised I would tell nobody, and I mustn't break a promise, but we must watch those men."

RUPERT SEES AN OLD BOX

They hear the angry men declare
" We've dug and dug, no treasure's there ! "

The men stamp off, the two friends run
To see just what the rogues have done.

" What luck they left this spade behind,
Let's dig and see what we can find."

Quite soon the spade on metal knocks,
It proves to be a brass-bound box.

Crawling even more cautiously, the two pals get near the Lion Rock in time to hear the men grumbling. " I'm worn out with digging," growls one of them. " We've dug nearly round the tree and found nothing. I don't believe there is any treasure there at all." " Oh, yes there is," says the skipper, " but it's getting too dark to see any more. We can try again at dawn." They stride heavily away. Then Rupert and Rollo creep up to see what they can of the digging. The gipsy boy becomes very excited. " That skipper said there was buried treasure here ! " he exclaims. " Yes," says Rupert. " It's here somewhere. Those men have dug most of the way round the tree. The treasure must be in the part they haven't touched. Look, they've left a spade, and it's not yet quite dark. Push it in and see if you can strike anything hard." Hurriedly the boy does so, and soon there is a sound of metal. Digging feverishly, he gradually reveals a very old brass-bound box.

RUPERT GETS A BIG SHOCK

Says Rupert, " Hide it right away,
They're coming back at break of day."

Amongst a grove of trees they creep
And very soon fall fast asleep.

Next morning when the pals awake,
Young Rollo gives the box a shake.

He lifts the lid and then he groans,
There's just a paper and some stones !

The old box is quickly uncovered, and by heaving together the two pals lift it from the hole. " It's jolly heavy," says Rollo breathlessly. " Yes, it's still full," adds Rupert. " I'm thankful we kept it away from those bad men." Tying some of the thinner cord round the box, they haul it away from the tree and into the shelter of the rocks and bushes. In the darkness they cannot see to do more, so they gather piles of leaves for pillows and settle down as comfortably as they can to sleep. At the first light of dawn Rupert wakes to find Rollo examining the box. " It opens easily enough," murmurs the boy. " The only fastening is a rod pushed through two staples." The lid creaks as it is lifted and inside they see a sheet of paper lying on top of a canvas bundle. Rupert takes the paper but before he can look at it there is a gasp from Rollo. " But this isn't treasure ! Look, there's nothing here but a heap of ordinary pebbles ! Is it the wrong box ? "

RUPERT HIDES AWAY TO WATCH

And so, beneath the selfsame tree,
The box is hidden hurriedly.

The work is hardly finished when
They see the three returning men !

The chums watch, keeping out of sight,
And hear the men shout in delight.

The rascals think the treasure's found
And soon towards the ship they're bound.

The shock of finding no treasure in the box makes Rupert forget the old piece of paper, which he folds and stuffs into his pocket. " There may be another box there," suggests Rollo. " Well, we've no time to do much now," sighs the little bear. " Anyway, there's no reason why those men shouldn't have this one." Quickly they take it back and rebury it and stamp the earth down flat. Hearing distant voices, they hurry into hiding. Soon the three men appear and head for the tree. Rupert and Rollo watch in great anxiety as the men continue their digging. Almost at once they find the box and the skipper gives a joyful shout. " There's no time to waste," he cries. " We must not be found here. Carry the box back to the ship. We can examine it and count the treasure there." " And what of those young rascals who have disappeared ?" asks one of the men. " I hope they've fallen overboard," growls the skipper. " That's nothing for us to worry about."

RUPERT'S FRIENDS ARRIVE

" We'll starve," says Rollo, " if we stay.
Let's call before they get away."

Says Rupert, " There's no need to fear,
Quite soon the others will be here."

Then from a height the ship they see.
" They've come ! " shouts Rupert, gleefully.

" Who ? " Rollo asks in great surprise.
" My friends ! " the little bear replies.

On reaching the small boat, one man pauses. " Supposing the little bear and the boy are on the island ? " he says. " Well, if they are let them stay and let them starve," snarls the skipper. " Come, push off." " I say," whispers Rollo, " oughtn't we to call out ? We *can't* be left here." " Oh, yes we can," chuckles Rupert. " Let's start climbing. The others should be here soon." " What others ? " cries Rollo. " I do *wish* you weren't so mysterious ! " Rupert leads the way upwards until they reach the topmost part of the island, from which he can see all the coastline. Suddenly he points. " Look ! Down by that headland. It's the other boat ! " he cries in great excitement. " They're here already." " Did you know that there would be another boat ? " exclaims Rollo. " Who is it ? Where is it from ? " But Rupert doesn't wait to answer. " Quickly, back to Lion Rock," he says, leading the way downhill again. " We must not miss them ! "

RUPERT TELLS HIS STORY

Then Rupert sees his friends below,
And greets them with a glad "Hullo !"

The admiral mutters angrily,
" Why, Rupert ! So you've followed me ! "

But Rupert says, " I've kept my word,
Wait till my story you have heard."

The rogues have sailed away at last,
Their ship is disappearing fast.

In their haste the two pals take a shorter way down the slope and find that it leads right on to Lion Rock. " There they are, down beside the tree. Hi, wait for us. We're coming," shouts Rupert. They scramble and slide the rest of the descent and are met by the two familiar figures. " Hullo, Admiral ! Hullo, Sam ! " calls out Rupert. " How pleased we are to see you ! " But the admiral looks both angry and bewildered. He faces Rupert with a frown. " How have you got here, little bear ? " he demands sternly. " You promised that you would keep my secret, and yet you have reached the treasure before us." " I did keep the secret," insists Rupert. " Listen, I'll tell you what happened." And he explains how he and Rollo stowed away with the bad men, and how he got ashore and how they found the box. " They've taken the box home. Look, there's their boat right out there," he adds. " But there was no treasure in it—only pebbles ! "

RUPERT REMEMBERS THE PAPER

The admiral says, " No use to stay. "
But Rupert cries, "Don't go away ! "

" I meant to give this sheet to you,
Perhaps it holds a secret clue."

" This paper shows," the admiral cries,
" Just where the buried treasure lies."

" It's in the Lion's Mouth up there.
You've saved the day, brave little bear."

The old admiral is terribly disappointed. " I can't make head or tail of it," he murmurs. " All that trouble and no reward ! " He stares at the trench round the tree. " If the box was there why was there no treasure in it ? Ah well, we can do no good here. Come on Sam, take your spade and let's be off." They trudge away, but Rupert stops suddenly. " Hi, wait," he says. " There was something else in the box, an old piece of paper. There it is. I stuffed it into my pocket and quite forgot about it. D'you think it means anything ? " The admiral gazes at the paper with growing excitement. " Why, now I understand ! This is the same code as I solved with my handyman," he cries. " It has altered everything. This is what it says : ' Ye who have sought thus far, know ye that my treasure is not here but lieth safe in the Lion's Mouth.' " He turns and points at the cleft in the rock above. " Little bear," he breathes, " you may have saved the day for us."

RUPERT FINDS A DEEP HOLE

How can they clamber up so high?
Then Rollo says, " The rope's nearby! "

With Sam in front they start to climb,
It's steep and takes them quite a time.

The Lion's mouth they've yet to gain,
It seems their efforts are in vain.

But Rupert searches all around
And finds a deep crack in the ground.

The message gives the little group a great thrill. " What luck you took the paper from the box and prevented that rascally skipper from getting it," chuckles the admiral. " Now we're full of new hope." " The treasure should still be there, but it looks almost impossible to get into the Lion's Mouth," says Rupert. " No," says Rollo. " It's not impossible. We've got the rope we brought from the ship. We can use that and try to reach the Lion's Mouth from above." Next minute Sailor Sam is leading them upwards, while the admiral waits below to watch progress. The others are soon on top of the Lion Rock. " I'd go over the edge if I could find something strong enough to fasten the rope to," murmurs Sam. " If only there were some trees up here." They search around and then Rupert calls out : " Look at this. There's a deep crack in the rock here. D'you think it leads down to the Lion's Mouth ? " The others hurry to him and gaze into the hole.

RUPERT LANDS ON THE LEDGE

" I'm small enough to wriggle through,"
He says, " So let me go, please do."

Soon Rupert's lowered, yard by yard,
He laughs and says, " It isn't hard."

He's nearly there, the mouth looks wide,
Another moment he's inside !

He searches till he finds the place—
A little pebble-covered space.

After peering into the cleft, Sailor Sam straightens up rather gloomily. " This won't do," he sighs. " The hole gets too narrow. I could never get through there." " But perhaps I could," says Rollo. " So could I," cries Rupert. " I'm the smallest. Besides I found the crack. Do let me try this ! " The sailor smiles. " Very well, little bear, you're a plucky one," he says. " You shall go." Tying the rope securely under Rupert's arms, he holds firmly to it and lowers Rupert into the darkness. The little bear worms his way down the cleft, avoiding the sharp edges of the rock, until the crack finishes. Then, calling to Sam to take his full weight, he swings the rest of the way and lands gently on the floor of the Lion's Mouth. Quickly he walks round and searches in every corner. " There doesn't seem to be anywhere to hide treasure here," he mutters. All at once he treads on something that is not solid rock. " Why are all these pebbles here ? " he wonders.

RUPERT DISCOVERS THE BAGS

Beneath the pebbles in the ground
Are bags which make a rattling sound.

He perches there, quite near the edge,
And waves a signal from the ledge.

The bags are thrown down one by one,
And soon his plucky task is done.

Then Sam pulls Rupert safely back,
Up through the dark and narrow crack.

Looking more closely, Rupert sees that there is a hole in the floor that has been filled with pebbles. " This must be the place," he breathes. Kneeling down, he scoops them away and soon he uncovers a small leather bag that clinks as he shakes it. Now he works feverishly and by the time the hole is emptied he has found twelve bags, all the same size. Carrying them to the edge of the Lion's Mouth, he shouts excitedly to the waiting admiral. Next he tosses the little leather bags down until all twelve are lying safely at the feet of the astonished old gentleman. Then, going back into the Lion's Mouth he shouts to Sailor Sam and is soon hauled back into the crack. Going up is harder than coming down, but at length he reaches his friends, who have heard his conversation with the admiral and want to know all about the wonderful ending to his search. " Well done ! " cries Sam, after hearing Rupert's news. " Won't my skipper be proud of you ! "

RUPERT EXPLAINS TO ROLLO

*" Those bags contain a splendid hoard,
Now we must get the jewels aboard."*

*The hunt has been a great success,
And brings the party happiness.*

*Cries Rupert, " Here's Jake and the boat,
I shall be glad when we're afloat."*

*" And now," says Rollo, " You can tell
The secret that you've kept so well."*

Rupert descends the slope while Sam and Rollo coil the rope and he is met by the delighted old gentleman. " Those bags were very small, weren't they ? " says Rupert. " There wasn't much treasure after all." " Oh yes, there was," says the admiral. " I find that there are lots of diamonds and emeralds in the bags, as well as some gold. So the find is worth a fortune !" Soon the others are down and in great glee Sailor Sam lashes the bags to his spade. Then they set off to rejoin Cornish Jake in their boat. In great excitement, the two pals race ahead of the others and soon they are all on board and setting off for home. As the islands grow small in the distance, Rupert is at last able to tell Rollo the whole story and to explain everything that has puzzled him. " After being away so long I shall have a lot of explaining to my Mummy when we reach Nutwood," he laughs. " So I hope that you and Sam and the Admiral will come and help me do it ! "

Rupert is very proud of his tank of fish which won a prize at the Nutwood Pets Club. Every day he sprinkles a pinch of special food on top of the water and watches while the fish swim to the surface in search of the tiny fragments. Not only are the fish very beautiful but Rupert has also made his tank bright and gay with water plants, coloured rocks and shells.

How to Make

A MODEL FISH TANK

Here is a picture of the completed model which can be made from a few odds and ends. For the tank you need a slender cardboard box, such as a cereal carton

When your model is held up to the light the fish will stand out brightly against the underwater background

NOW READ HOW TO DO IT

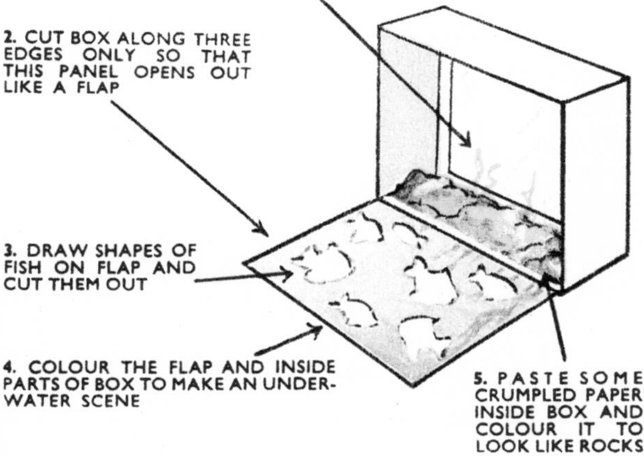

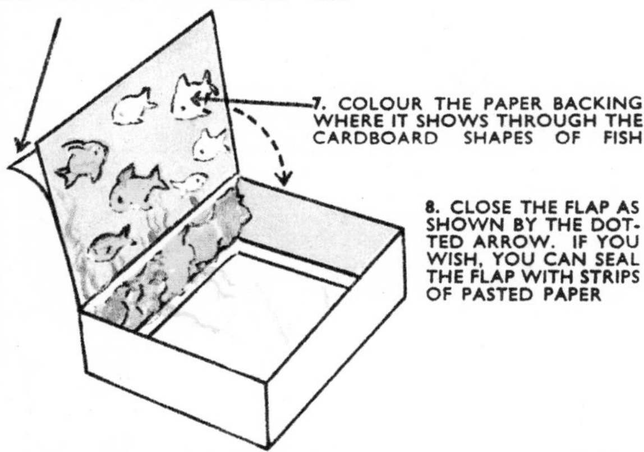

1. CUT OUT THE CENTRE PART OF ONE BIG PANEL LEAVING ½ INCH FRAME ALL ROUND. PASTE A PIECE OF CLEAR CELLOPHANE ON INSIDE OF OPENING
2. CUT BOX ALONG THREE EDGES ONLY SO THAT THIS PANEL OPENS OUT LIKE A FLAP
3. DRAW SHAPES OF FISH ON FLAP AND CUT THEM OUT
4. COLOUR THE FLAP AND INSIDE PARTS OF BOX TO MAKE AN UNDERWATER SCENE
5. PASTE SOME CRUMPLED PAPER INSIDE BOX AND COLOUR IT TO LOOK LIKE ROCKS

6. PASTE GREASEPROOF PAPER (OR PART OF A THIN PAPER BAG) ON OUTSIDE OF BOX TO COVER FLAP
7. COLOUR THE PAPER BACKING WHERE IT SHOWS THROUGH THE CARDBOARD SHAPES OF FISH
8. CLOSE THE FLAP AS SHOWN BY THE DOTTED ARROW. IF YOU WISH, YOU CAN SEAL THE FLAP WITH STRIPS OF PASTED PAPER

9. COMPLETE YOUR MODEL FISH TANK BY COVERING THE OUTSIDE OF THE BOX WITH PASTED-ON PIECES OF COLOURED PAPER

KEY TO THE PICTURE. 1. Red Swordtail. 2. Angel Fish. 3. Zebra Fish. 4. Black Molly. 5. Parrot Fish. 6. Butterfly Fish. 7. Harlequin Fish. 8. Tiger Barb.

HOW TO MAKE RUPERT'

If you would like to make the glider which you read abou
"Rupert and the Cracker Jack", here are the instructi
A piece of light, strong paper is needed—typewriter pa
about 10 in. by 8 in. is just right. Lay the top edge aga
each of the sides to give the two folds from A to C in Fig
Turn the paper over and lay AA against CC to make the
BB. Turn the paper back again, bring the points marke
together, letting the edge AA come down to CC (Fig. 2

Next take the points AA up to D (Fig. 3) and fold the
sides AF, BF, AE and BE in turn to the middle line mak
the creases shown by the dotted lines. Now take the two s
AF and BF and, as far as possible, put them at the same t
against the line AB. This leaves the point F standing

Treat AE and BE in the same way to give Fig. 4. Press
folds firmly making sure that the upright folds come exa
to E and F. (*Instructions continued on facing page*)

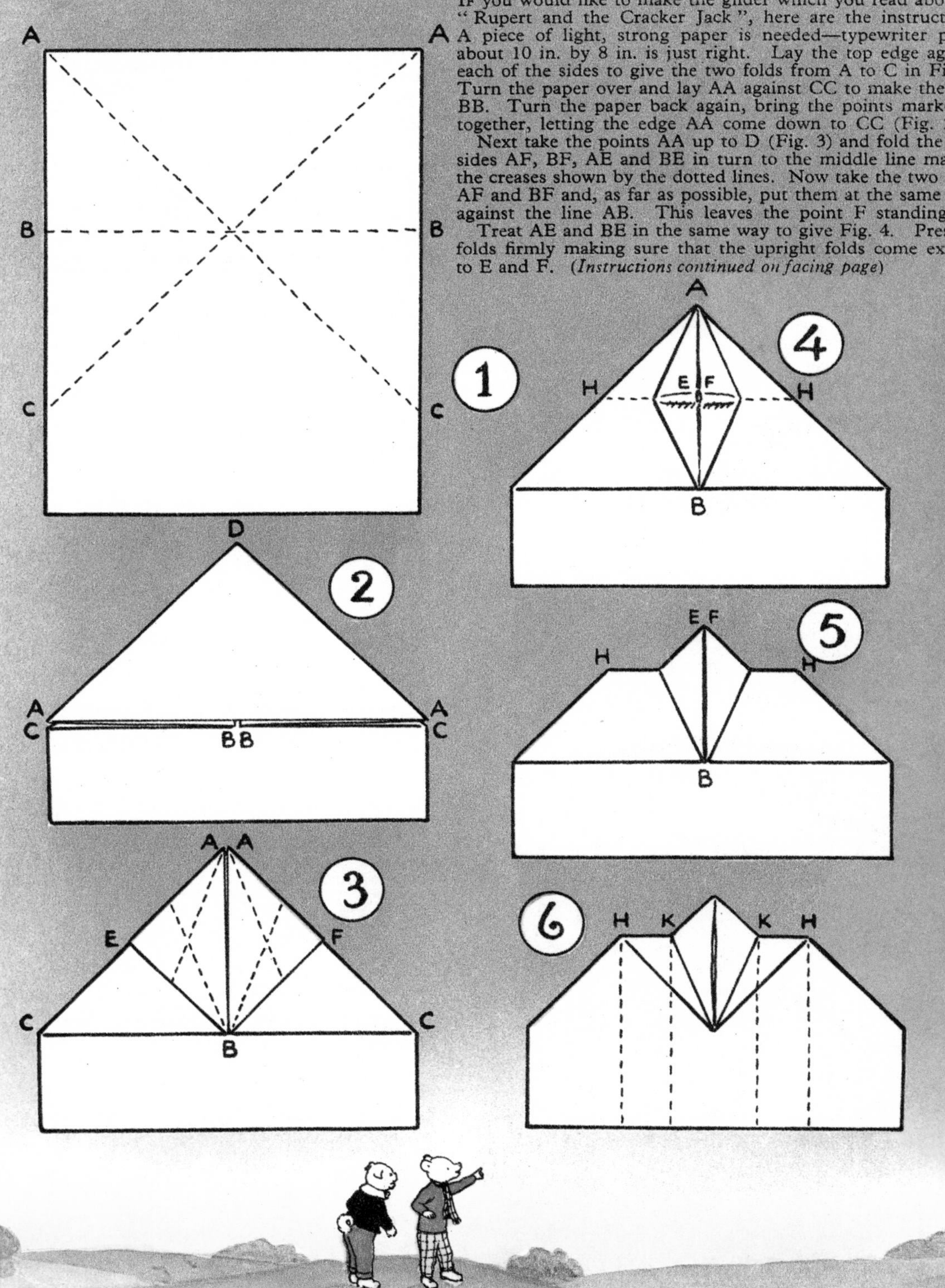

'OLDED PAPER GLIDER

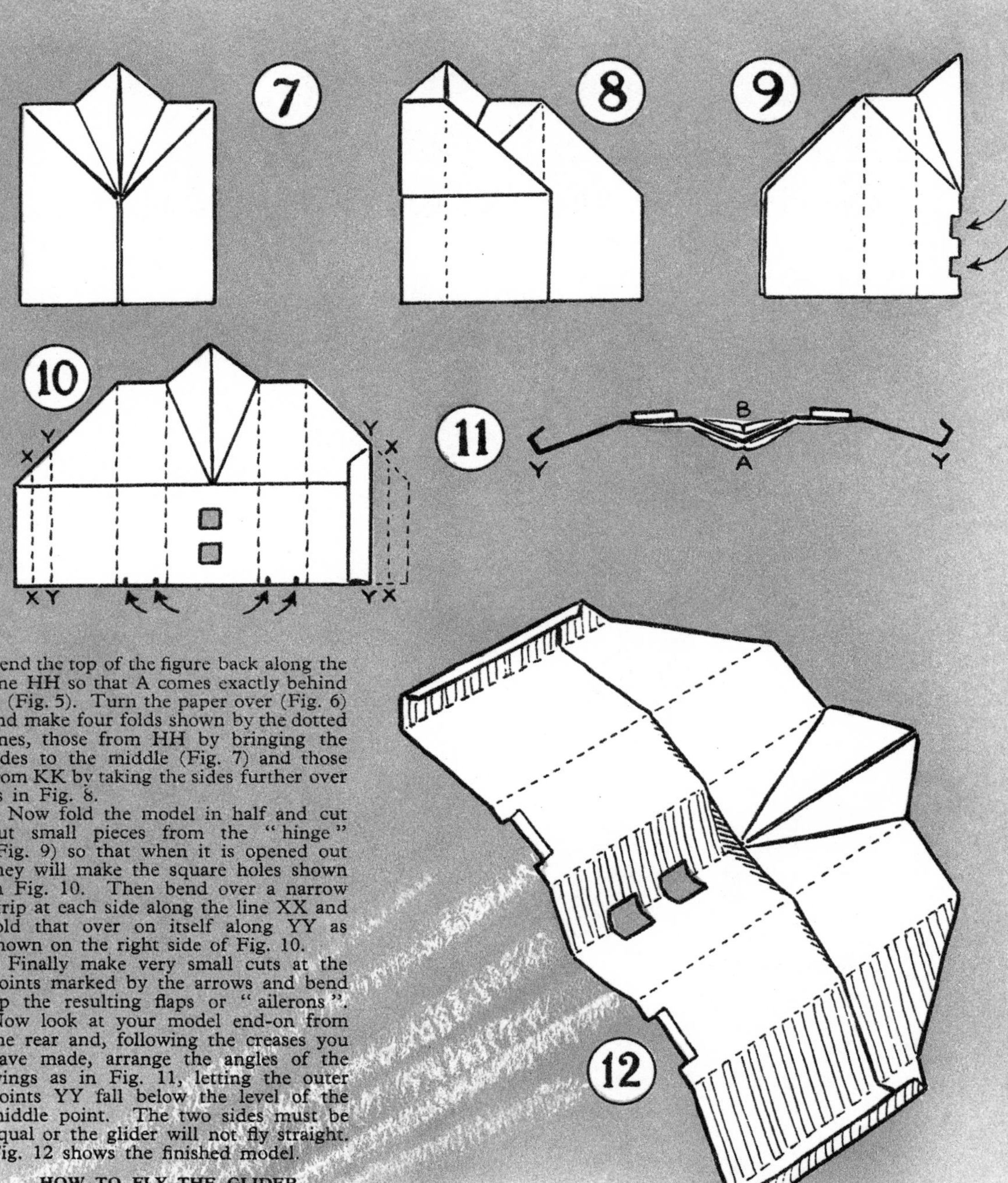

Bend the top of the figure back along the line HH so that A comes exactly behind B (Fig. 5). Turn the paper over (Fig. 6) and make four folds shown by the dotted lines, those from HH by bringing the sides to the middle (Fig. 7) and those from KK by taking the sides further over as in Fig. 8.

Now fold the model in half and cut out small pieces from the " hinge " (Fig. 9) so that when it is opened out they will make the square holes shown in Fig. 10. Then bend over a narrow strip at each side along the line XX and fold that over on itself along YY as shown on the right side of Fig. 10.

Finally make very small cuts at the points marked by the arrows and bend up the resulting flaps or " ailerons ". Now look at your model end-on from the rear and, following the creases you have made, arrange the angles of the wings as in Fig. 11, letting the outer points YY fall below the level of the middle point. The two sides must be equal or the glider will not fly straight. Fig. 12 shows the finished model.

HOW TO FLY THE GLIDER

Hold it by the point A which is now underneath. Launch it gently forward and it will glide a long way. If you use rather more force the little flaps will swing it straight upwards. If you throw it harder still it will loop the loop. It is interesting to try slightly different creases and other shapes for the holes in the middle.

RUPERT and the WIND WHISTLE

As soon as the whistle is blown a surprising adventure begins for the little bear and his chums

How Rupert hopes that he may go
To play in all the lovely snow!

" Your gloves and overcoat you'll need,
The wind is very cold indeed."

" I'll take my sledge out for some fun.
Perhaps I'll find a nice steep run."

Off Rupert goes, and soon he sees
Some fresh-made footmarks near the trees.

IT is midwinter. Snow is lying thick on the fields and a sharp wind is blowing. "My, it's jolly cold, but it looks a nice day," thinks Rupert as he opens the front door and peeps out. " I wonder if Mummy will let me go and play now that the snow has stopped falling." He trots into the parlour where Mrs. Bear is busy cleaning a grate. " Mummy," says Rupert. " May I go out this morning ? " " Yes, it will do you good," says his mummy. " But be sure to keep warm. Put on your overcoat and gloves." After wrapping himself up well, Rupert runs outside. " It's just right for my sledge," he says. " I'll take it with me and have some fun." He fetches his sledge from the tool-shed and as he makes his way towards the nearest slopes he shivers in the biting air. " Oh dear, I don't fancy sledging in this wind," he thinks. He pauses for a moment and stares at the ground. " Hullo, there's someone else about," he says. " And that's a sledge track too."

Rupert and the Wind Whistle

RUPERT SEES A STRANGE WALLET

He follows in the tracks until
He catches up with school-mate Bill.

" Hark," says Rupert. " What's that sound ? "
They listen, as they gaze around.

Cries Willie Mouse, as they draw near,
" Just look what I have picked up here ! "

" This wallet has been left behind,
Yet no one's footsteps can I find."

Rupert follows the tracks and soon discovers that they have been made by Bill Badger, who is standing and flapping his arms as he tries to keep warm. " Hullo, Rupert. Did you ever know such a cold day ? " says Bill, with his teeth chattering. " I thought it would be good fun on my sledge, but I've changed my mind." " So have I," replies Rupert. " We should freeze if we tried them. What else shall we play—snowballs ? " Before Bill can answer, thev hear someone calling them from another direction. They find that the call has come from their pal Willie the mouse, who is standing not far away and waving something at them. " Look what I've picked up," he shouts. " It was lying just here." And he shows them a small round wallet. " It's very odd," he adds. " The wallet was on top of the snow, but there were no foot-marks anywhere near except mine. No one can have passed." The three friends stand and look at each other silently.

RUPERT FINDS SOME PILLS

" It may be ice, or else a sweet,
I wonder if it's good to eat."

Then Willie squeals and gasps, " Oh dear!
My tummy feels so very queer!"

Cries Rupert, as they start to run,
" Just look what Willie Mouse has done!"

" Don't worry! I'm not going to freeze!
I feel so warm, I don't need these!"

At length Rupert opens the wallet. " Perhaps there's something inside that will tell us whose it is," he murmurs. " Hello, there are three little beads of glass. No, they're not glass—I believe they're made of ice." He takes one and gazes at it. " Perhaps it's a sweet," says Willie, grabbing it and popping it in his mouth. Next minute he is dancing about and hugging himself and making comical faces. " Ooo-hoo-hoo! Ow-ow!" he squeaks. " I do feel funny! I'm tingling all over and I don't know whether I'm freezing or boiling!" Gradually Willie calms down and Rupert realises how cold he has been getting. " Come on, let's run about for a bit," he suggests. With Bill he starts off briskly. Then he notices that Willie is slowly taking off his thick scarf and overcoat. " Hi, what are you doing?" cries Rupert. " You'll freeze." " Freeze! I shan't freeze—I don't even feel cold," says Willie. " I've suddenly begun to feel warm. Do you think it was that sweet?"

RUPERT AND BILL FEEL WARM

*" Two magic sweets are left, you know.
We'll see if they will make* us *glow."*

*Says Bill, " We've done the same as you !
That's why we're feeling warmer too ! "*

*And then the chums together make
Towards a partly frozen lake.*

*" This wallet has an inner part,
Let's look inside before we start."*

Rupert and Bill gaze wonderingly at their little pal who is walking away to fetch their sledges. " There must have been some magic in the sweet," says Rupert. " There are two more in this wallet. Shall we try them and see if they have the same effect ? " " Yes, rather, I'd give anything to feel a bit warmer," says Bill, shivering. So they chew them and in a few moments they too are unable to feel the cold. " This is amazing," cries Bill. " Now that we don't feel the cold we shall be able to use our sledges without freezing." " Oo, topping ! Will you take me with you ? " says Willie. " Let's slide down to that lake and find out why one end of it has not frozen over." " Jolly good idea," agrees Rupert, " but we shall not need our overcoats. Let's leave them in this hollow tree, and I'll leave this mysterious wallet with them." Then he pauses. " I say," he calls. " I believe I can feel something else in this wallet. There must be an inner pocket that we missed."

RUPERT DISCOVERS A WHISTLE

Cries Rupert, " Doesn't this look nice ?
A little whistle, made of ice."

Bill Badger blows, and then they hear
The whistle's note, so thin and clear.

" Look ! What's happening over there ? "
Shouts Willie, as they stand and stare.

Though Rupert scrambles down the hill,
The others stand there watching still.

The little bear quickly finds the opening of the secret pocket and takes something out of it. " It looks like a tiny whistle," says Rupert. " What a lovely little thing." " And it seems to be made of ice like those sweets," adds Willie. " I wonder if it would make a noise," says Bill. "Let's try it." He blows, and from the whistle there comes a thin, clear note that echoes all round and seems to make the air tremble. After Bill has had his turn Willie takes the whistle and again there comes that thin, beautiful note. " I say, doesn't it sound topping ! Do let me have a go," says Rupert. But before he can put it to his lips there is an anxious call from the little mouse. " Hi, look what's happening ! " There is a dull moaning noise in the distance, and huge clouds billow up over the horizon. " Ooo ! Something awful is coming," Rupert shouts. " Let's get out of its way ! " Pocketing the whistle, he quickly slides down the snow into the shelter of the bank.

Rupert and the Wind Whistle

RUPERT'S FRIENDS DISAPPEAR

" What's in that cloud ? " cries Rupert Bear,
" I thought I saw my friends up there ! "

" Where they have gone, I do not know ! "
Gasps Rupert, sprawling in the snow.

The little bear feels very dazed.
The mystery leaves him amazed.

" To see this calm and peaceful scene,
You'd think the wind had never been ! "

Rupert crouches near the tree and waits for the others to join him, but Bill Badger and Willie seem to be so terrified that they cannot move. The sky grows rapidly darker, the distant noise swells to a great roar and the air fills with lumps of snow and ice as a giant wind crashes against the bank. For an instant Rupert thinks he can see two forms swept away in the cloud above him, but next minute it is all over and he is nearly buried by the mass of snow that follows the wind.

Scrambling out of the heap of snow, Rupert leans against the tree and gazes around. The storm of wind that came and went so suddenly has left him breathless and dazed. Of his two pals there is no sign. " Surely Bill and Willie were here a minute ago," he mutters. " What can have happened to them ? Can I be dreaming ? " Digging into the snow, he uncovers his sledge and slowly drags it to the top of the slope. In every direction the countryside looks calm and peaceful again !

RUPERT HAS A TUMBLE

So Rupert gets upon his sledge
And skims towards the water's edge.

The sledge then hits a grassy clump
And Rupert Bear gets such a bump!

" The snow is melting on the ground! "
Cries Rupert, as he looks around.

He gathers firewood while he waits
In hope of meeting his playmates.

After a long pause, Rupert tries to pull himself together. " Perhaps Bill and Willie have gone ahead to the lake," he whispers. " I'll go and see." Another moment and he is on his sledge careering down the slope towards that end of the lake still unfrozen. Suddenly he reaches a spot where there is no snow, and the nose of the sledge buries itself in a patch of soft earth, throwing Rupert head over heels. " Well, here's an extraordinary thing," he mutters, picking himself up rather shakily. " Everywhere else it's the coldest day of the winter, yet half of the lake is not even frozen, and here's a patch of ground without much snow." He looks for his chums, but cannot find them. " I'll wait awhile in case they turn up," he decides. So he spends his time gathering sticks to take home for firewood. Using a length of cord he has found in his pocket, he lashes the bundle of wood to his sledge, and he is about to move on when he hears a weak unhappy sound not far away.

RUPERT MEETS JACK FROST

Then Rupert hears a mournful moan,
And sees Jack Frost there, all alone.

" You do look ill, it's plain to see,
I'd better take you home with me."

" Is this a cold that makes me wheeze ?
And was that horrid thing a sneeze ? "

" My sledge is close by—you can ride,"
Says Rupert, walking by Jack's side.

Making his way silently into the wood and guided by sound, Rupert discovers a small figure sitting on a low branch and moaning dismally. " Why, it's Jack Frost," he says. " What ever is the matter ? " At the sound of his voice the other drops to the ground and crouches near a tree. " Oh, Rupert," says Jack. " I'm so ill, I can hardly see or breathe and my work's not finished, half the lake is not frozen." " So that's the reason for it," says Rupert. " Come, let me take you back to my home." As soon as Jack Frost gets up he is shaken by a tremendous sneeze. " Oh dear, oh dear, what on earth is the matter with me ? " he snuffles. " Cheer up," says Rupert. " I don't think you're very ill. That sneeze means you've caught a cold, that's all." " Oh my, was that a sneeze ? " wheezes Jack. " I've never had one before, and I don't like it a bit. I thought I was terribly ill." " Nobody likes a cold," says Rupert. " Come on, I'll take you home on my sledge."

RUPERT GIVES A HELPING HAND

Poor Jack is feeling very ill,
So Rupert drags him up the hill.

There at the door stands Mrs. Bear,
She cries, " Now who have you got there ? "

" I'll wrap you in this blanket tight,"
Says Rupert, " then you'll be all right."

" Now just see what my Mummy's got !
A lovely drink, all steaming hot."

Jack Frost sprawls wearily on the top of the bundle of wood, and Rupert pulls him uphill away from the lake. On the higher ground they find the air bitterly cold, and by the time the cottage is reached Jack is shivering so much that he cannot walk, and Rupert has to carry him to where Mrs. Bear is standing in the cottage doorway. When she hears the story she bustles away to make a hot drink for Jack, and she tells Rupert to wrap him warmly in a blanket and to put him on the couch.

" It's really all my own fault," croaks Jack. " I never felt the cold before because I live on ice pills. I carry a few in my wallet. When the effect of one wears off I take another, but today I lost my precious wallet, and I've no idea where it fell. If only I could find it I'd be all right in a minute." Rupert stares at him. " Did you mean a little round wallet ? " he asks. But at that moment Mrs. Bear interrupts them with a steaming drink. " Sip it until it has all gone," she says.

RUPERT EXPLAINS TO JACK

*" We found three pills, which looked like ice,
We ate them, and they tasted nice."*

*" If you have found my whistle too,
I may be rescued, thanks to you."*

*" Yes, that's the whistle, now please go
And find a nice high spot, and blow ! "*

*" Jack told me what it is he needs,
So may I help him ? " Rupert pleads.*

To Mrs. Bear's surprise, Jack Frost refuses the warm drink. " I've never had anything hot in my life," he says. Then Rupert chimes in. " Bill and Willie have found a wallet that must have been yours," he says. " There were three pills in it, and we each had one. After that we didn't feel cold any more, so we took our overcoats off. There was a tiny whistle in the wallet, too, and——" At that Jack scrambles off the couch. " My whistle ! " he gasps. " Is it safe ? " At Jack's words Rupert puts his hand in his pocket and produces the whistle. " You've got it, you've got it," wheezes Jack. " Quick, you must go to some high spot and blow it and the wind will take you to my home, and my father, King Frost, will give you more ice pills for me. It's terribly cold there, and I couldn't stand it now, but you could." Mrs. Bear looks rather solemn when Rupert asks permission to go. " It will be all right, really," he pleads. " Jack would never send me if it was dangerous."

RUPERT BLOWS THE WHISTLE

" That little hill looks fairly high,
I'll climb up there and have a try."

Then, standing on the lonely hill,
He blows a note that's clear and shrill.

A sudden swirl of snow and sleet,
Sweeps Rupert Bear right off his feet

He flies through darkness like the night,
Where moon and stars are shining bright.

After much hesitation Mrs. Bear allows Rupert to start on his journey. He makes for the high point at the beginning of Nutwood Common. The farther he gets from his home the lonelier he feels, and as he stands on top of the little hill he is not very happy. " I suppose Jack Frost really knows what he is talking about," he murmurs. " I wish one of my pals could be here too." However, at length he screws up his courage and blows the whistle. The clear, beautiful note dies away in the distance, and Rupert quickly puts the tiny thing back in his pocket. Hardly has he done so when great billowing clouds appear over the horizon and rush towards him driven by a sudden wind. Before he can think what to do he is swept off his feet into the air with a swirl of powdered snow. Up and up he goes away from the white fields of Nutwood, away from the daylight. The force of the wind sweeps him on into darkness lit by stars and a crescent moon.

Rupert and the Wind Whistle

RUPERT REACHES THE PALACE

The journey ends and Rupert lands,
Just where an angry sentry stands.

As soon as Rupert scrambles near,
The sentry cries, " How came you here ? "

The sentry frowns, and with a glare
Drives on the puzzled little bear.

" I took the whistle, gave a blow,
And here I am ! That's all I know ! "

A sudden glow appears far ahead, and Rupert feels himself dropping down until he lands quite gently in a pile of snow. Ahead of him is a glittering castle of ice, and on the frozen steps stands a grim little guard holding a slender spear. Floundering through the deep, soft snow, Rupert manages to reach the steps. " Halt ! Who are you ? " says the guard, frowning. " Have you the password ? How came you here ? And why ? " Rupert tries hard to explain, but the little guard hustles him down a long corridor. " You must go before the Court Chamberlain," he growls. Soon they are facing another, larger figure who glares in anger. " This is the palace of King Frost, and it is being invaded by strange creatures ! " he rasps. " How ever did you get here ? " " Please, I blew the whistle and I just came," quavers Rupert. " Tcha ! That's what the others said," growls the Chamberlain. " Lock him up and report him to the King ! "

Rupert and the Wind Whistle

RUPERT GREETS HIS FRIENDS

But Rupert's words are all in vain,
The guards take him away again.

He's in an icy, narrow room
That scares him with its air of gloom.

And as he hears them slam the door,
He sees his Nutwood friends once more.

" So this is where you went, you two !
I'm so glad I've discovered you ! "

A bell rings and another guard appears, and together they hurry Rupert into a distant ice tower. On the way he makes one more effort. " Oh, please do listen," he begs. " I've come here because of Jack Frost, who is lying ill at Nutwood, and he asked me to come and get him some more of his . . ." But the others interrupt roughly and, forcing him into a bare, gloomy apartment, they tell him sternly to be quiet. As the door clangs behind him Rupert peers round into the gloom and, to his astonishment, he hears voices. " Why, it's Rupert ! It's Rupert ! " And from the darkness his two pals Willie Mouse and Bill Badger rush across to greet him. The ice floor is too slippery for Willie, who topples over, but he is soon up again. " So this is where you got to when you blew the whistle ! " cries the little bear. " My, but I'm glad to see you ! " " But where are we ? " says Bill. " Did you blow that whistle, too ? What's going to happen to us ? "

RUPERT IS TAKEN TO THE KING

" We can't escape, it seems to me,
There's no way out that I can see."

As Rupert turns and hears a shout,
A sentry waves and calls him out.

" This ledge is frozen, I might slide,"
Thinks Rupert when he gets outside.

At last they take him to the King,
Who cries, " Now tell me everything ! "

Rupert hastily tells his friends all that has happened since they disappeared, of his meeting with Jack Frost and his strange journey. " Yes, we took that journey, too. It was awful. And how are we going to get away ? " asks Willie as they lead the way from the gloom into another room, where there is a little window. " There's no escape here," says Bill, " but we must do something. The effect of those pills is wearing off. We're beginning to freeze." A sudden noise interrupts them as the guard enters and shouts for Rupert. Taking the little bear from his friends two guards march him away. Silently they slide round dangerous ledges, in and out of towers, across bridges, and into the royal rooms. King Frost looks at him gloomily. " I do not understand this invasion of my Palace," he says sternly. " Where are you from ? What brought you here ? How is it that you are not frozen ? And why did you mention my son Jack ? "

RUPERT TELLS HIS STORY

So Rupert does as he is told,
And tells how Jack has caught a cold.

" I got this whistle from poor Jack,
And I must take some ice pills back."

The King commands, the guards then run
To fetch a wallet for his son.

" Jack left the whistle in my care.
I'll keep it," says the little bear.

Rupert goes forward eagerly and tells his story of how Jack Frost lost his wallet, caught a bad cold, and how he was found. " Please, he feels dreadful," adds the little bear. " He told me just how to get here because he must have some more ice pills, or he may never be better again. Bill Badger and Willie had already blown the whistle before they knew what it was, and they're here, too. Look, here's the whistle." He pulls it from his pocket and King Frost gazes at it keenly. " Tis true," he breathes. " Tis my son Jack's own whistle." Rupert stands by the throne while King Frost issues his orders briskly. " The little bear must be telling the truth," he says. " My son is in trouble. Hurry, fetch a new wallet for him and some more ice pills. This brave little messenger from Nutwood shall not be kept waiting." Several small guards run off at top speed to obey, while Rupert tucks the whistle back into his pocket and stays to answer the King's many questions.

RUPERT BRINGS GOOD NEWS

" Can my friends also have a pill ?
For Willie's cold, and so is Bill."

The King explains, " To make amends,
I've sent the guard to fetch your friends."

" Cheer up ! " cries Rupert. " Don't look glum !
Here are the pills—they gave me some ! "

" So from the wallet, I'll take three,
For Bill, for Willie, and for me."

In a very short time two of the guards return. " We thought the little bear might like a wallet for himself," says one of them. The other offers a big supply of pills in a box. " That's a fine lot," says Rupert. " The effect of the ice pill I took is wearing off and I'm beginning to feel chilly. And my pals Bill and Willie are very cold and miserable. Could they be fetched to go home with me ? " The king smiles. " After what you've done I can deny you nothing," he says. And while the guards run off he shows Rupert the beauties of the palace. Soon there is the sound of footsteps and a guard returns bringing Bill and Willie with him. The two friends look very glum and are shivering. " Cheer up," says Rupert. " You'll soon be smiling again. King Frost has given us a new wallet for Jack and one for me, and look, here are some more ice pills. We'll take one each and then we shan't feel cold on the homeward journey. Let's ask King Frost how we can get back."

Rupert and the Wind Whistle

RUPERT SAYS GOODBYE

The chums hear King Frost's parting speech.
And then he bids farewell to each.

A massive tower comes in sight,
" My word ! " gasps Rupert. " What a height ! "

" I hope the guard knows how to stop.
We must be getting near the top ! "

They climb out with the greatest care,
For it is dangerous up there.

Rupert introduces Bill and Willie to King Frost and they look very nervous. " I ought to be very angry with you," says the King, " but the little bear has explained everything and he is doing his utmost to help my son. You shall go home with him and go quickly." A guard takes them away while the King watches and waves from the battlements. Again they march through buildings, and over a bridge towards a high tower with a flat top. " My word, what a height," thinks Rupert.

Inside the strange tower Rupert finds that climbing is not so difficult as it looks. The guard makes them stand in the middle of the floor, then he presses a button and part of the floor moves rapidly upwards to a great height, until they reach a short staircase leading to a trap-door on to the roof. " Ooo, what a dangerous sort of place," quavers Bill as he pops his head out. " Come on and be careful," says the guard. " The little bear must blow the whistle as he did to get here."

RUPERT STARTS FOR HOME

" Wait till I've gone, please," says the guard,
" Then take the whistle, and blow hard."

They hear the whistle's echo fade,
It makes the three pals feel afraid.

They hold their breath and wait to meet
The wind which sweeps them off their feet.

Head over heels, away they go,
Above the mountains white with snow.

While Rupert stuffs the wallets in his pocket the guard tells the three friends what they must do. Then he dodges back down the staircase. " Don't begin until I've shut this trapdoor," he laughs. " I don't want to get carried off too ! " In a moment he is gone and the three friends feel very lonely. " Let's get it over," says Rupert quietly, and blows a shrill blast on the whistle and then puts it back in his pocket. They all hold hands to keep up their courage while they wait.

Although the three pals know what is going to happen they cannot help feeling scared as the giant wind approaches. Again they are caught and whirled off the flat top of the tower. Almost at once King Frost's wonder palace is left far behind and Rupert finds himself turning over and over, high above snow-covered mountains, out of the cold light and into darkness. At length another kind of light appears far ahead. " That must be home," gasps Rupert, by now almost breathless.

RUPERT HURRIES TO JACK FROST

When they land safely by the tree
Their coats inside the trunk they see.

Then Rupert says, " I must make haste,
There isn't any time to waste."

" I'm back again at last, Jack Frost !
You must have thought that I'd got lost ! "

" Oh, thank you, Rupert ! I've been ill,
But I'll recover, with a pill."

The three friends drop down until, with great suddenness, they land in a snowdrift. Struggling to their feet, they look around. " Why, this is where we started from ! " says Willie. " See, here's the hollow tree and our overcoats are still in it." " How splendid," laughs Rupert. " The whistle has worked again. I must hurry to Jack Frost. I'll tell you what, Bill, your sledge is still under this snow. If you get it out you can bring all the coats on it." Making haste as best he can, Rupert reaches the cottage and hurries to the side of Jack Frost. The little figure opens one eye and gives a miserable snuffle. " Oh, dear, are you still here ? " he croaks. " Aren't you going to blow that whistle ? " " But I've blown it," laughs Rupert. " Look what I've brought you. A new wallet. And some more of your precious pills and, what's more, here is your precious whistle." " Goodness, what a pal you are," wheezes Jack as he takes the wallet and opens it feverishly.

RUPERT SURPRISES HIS MUMMY

" I'm well again, I do declare ! "
Shouts Jack, and leaps into the air.

" I'm off to freeze that lake ! Hooray ! "
Jack chuckles, then he bounds away.

" He hadn't time to stay, you see ! "
Laughs Rupert. " Now let's have some tea ! "

Says Mrs. Bear, " Those pills won't do,
An overcoat's the thing for you."

Jack Frost swallows one of the ice pills and fastens the new wallet securely to his belt. There is a moment's pause, and then he grabs his hat, flings off the blankets and leaps into the air. " That's amazing," he cries. " I'm well, I'm well again ! Thank you Rupert. But for you I should never have got to my home again. Now I must go and finish my work of freezing that lake." In a twinkling he is bounding away before the astonished eyes of Bill and Willie, who are approaching the cottage with their sledge. " That was Jack Frost. I don't suppose we'll see him again until next winter," says Rupert. " Anyway, let's tell Mummy all about it. I expect she'll give us some tea." Mrs. Bear listens with growing surprise to the story of the journey and looks very suspiciously at the ice pills. " M-m, I hear what you say," she murmurs slowly, " but I don't believe in keeping warm by magic. It's safer to wear an overcoat."

RUPERT'S Colouring Contest is open to all readers up to the age of 15. Every boy and girl—even the youngest—will have a chance of winning one of the splendid money prizes, so try your very best when you colour the Contest picture, which is on the next page. Read the rules carefully and be sure to post your entry before the closing date, 31st January, 1958.

How the Prizes will be Awarded

Entries will be divided into four groups

GROUP 1 . . . Boys and Girls up to 6 years

GROUP 2 . . . Boys and Girls 7-9 years

GROUP 3 . . . Boys and Girls 10-12 years

GROUP 4 . . . Boys and Girls 13-15 years

In each of the four groups the following prizes will be awarded

BOYS		GIRLS	
1st . . .	**£10**	1st . . .	**£10**
2nd . . .	**£5**	2nd . . .	**£5**
3rd . . .	**£3**	3rd . . .	**£3**
4th . . .	**£2**	4th . . .	**£2**
and £1 prizes for the five next best efforts		and £1 prizes for the five next best efforts	

All prizes will be forwarded not later than 31st March, 1958. A list of prize-winners will be sent on application to RUPERT'S COLOURING CONTEST RESULT, 26-29 Poppins Court, London, E.C.4.

Rules of the Contest

1. Colour the picture as nicely as you can with paints, crayons, coloured inks or chalks.

2. Age, skill and neatness will be taken into consideration.

3. Complete the entry form with your age, name and address and indicate Boy or Girl. Do not detach the form from the picture. A parent, guardian or teacher must certify that the colouring is entirely your own work.

4. Send your picture together with the entry form in a sealed envelope bearing a 2½d. stamp. Insufficient postage will disqualify the entrant. Address the envelope to RUPERT'S COLOURING CONTEST, 26-29 Poppins Court, London, E.C.4.

5. All entries must be received on or before **31st January, 1958.** No entry will be accepted after this date.

6. Children of employees of Beaverbrook Newspapers Ltd., and associated companies are not allowed to compete.

7. The judges' decision is final and no correspondence will be allowed. In no circumstances will competitors' entries be returned.

SPECIAL PRIZES FOR OVERSEAS READERS !

Boys and girls who live abroad can also enter for the Contest. Entries must be posted to RUPERT'S COLOURING CONTEST, 26-29 Poppins Court, London, E.C.4, to arrive not later than 31st March, 1958. Special prizes will be awarded to overseas winners—1st, £10; 2nd, £5; 3rd, £3; 4th, £2; and £1 prizes for the five next best efforts. There are two groups, one for boys and one for girls, making the total prize-money £50. All overseas readers up to the age of 15 may enter. Add date of birth to entry form.

THE PICTURE TO COLOUR IS ON THE NEXT PAGE

If you wish to enter for the Contest remove page by cutting along this dotted line. It will not spoil your book.

RUPERT'S COLOURING CONTEST

Rupert and his chums find a cave to explore

ENTRY FORM *for* **RUPERT'S COLOURING CONTEST**

I have read the rules and agree to accept the judges' decision as final

FULL NAME..
(Print capital letters)

FULL POSTAL ADDRESS...

....**AGE (at 31st Jan., 1958)**......

I certify that this entry is the unaided work of the above entrant.

Signature of Parent, Guardian or Teacher..

DO NOT DETACH THIS ENTRY FORM FROM THE PICTURE

Put a large cross to indicate boy or girl

BOY ....

GIRL ....

SOLUTIONS TO PUZZLES

Rupert's Country Puzzle (*See Pages* 28 *and* 29)
The little creatures' homes shown in the circles are— 1. Robin's nest. 2. Harvest mouse's nest. 3. Molehill. 4. Squirrels' hollow. 5. Rabbit's burrow. 6. Hedgehog's nest.

Rupert's Funfair Puzzle (*See Pages* 52 *and* 53)
There are nine circus animals hidden in the picture—a chimpanzee, two monkeys, a kangaroo, a horse, two seals, an elephant and a giraffe.
Look at the picture again if you did not find them all the first time.

*Published by Oldbourne Book Co. Ltd., Fleet Street, E.C.4
and printed by L.T.A.Robinson, Ltd.*